Mysterious Ways

Mysterious Ways
A Collection of Quirky Tales

Jeff Laurents

Bridge House

British Library Cataloguing in Publication Data
A Record of this Publication is available from the British
Library

ISBN 978-1-914199-04-2

This edition published 2021 by Bridge House Publishing
Manchester, England

Contents

Introduction

Thirteen short stories by Jeff Laurents, all completed during a highly creative burst of writing energy and all revealing the author's penchant for the macabre and his interest in the supernatural and failed science and technology.

Meet David Hetherington, who wants to extend his life span so that he can meet his own true love, and having died in an accident, is reborn after following a special medical regime prescribed by his doctor.

Shudder at the gruesome imagery in *An Apple A Day*, *Horror Hammer* and *Animal Tragic*. Influenced, amongst other works, by the novels of Stephen King and the films of Alfred Hitchcock, Jeff revels in appealing to the audience's fascination with horror, with confronting the experience of fear. Many of us approach horror stories wanting to discover what happens next, even though we know it will almost certainly be abhorrent.

In *Johnny Lucifer*, Jeff plays with the supernatural in a story featuring vampires, though the narrative is laced with his sense of humour, as when Johnny remarks to his friend 'Arnie', who he turned into a vampire many years before, "You used to be a thief. Now you are the Member of Parliament for Hampstead." The supernatural also features in *Time Flies* and *Queen Victoria's Ghost*, both of which climax surprisingly.

Jeff's characters are not ordinary people; they invariably have extreme characteristics or ambitions, as we can see in Mimsie Fotheringey, "a nasty piece of work" who uses men, and when she is bored, then loses them. Or take the scientist, Charles Fortescue, experimenting on his baby son to further his own ambitions, and The Great Maldini, driven to be the most successful stage magician of all time, but who finds himself locked in a time warp, most likely for all time!

There is very little in these stories that can be said to be ordinary, which is one reason for their intriguing power.

Mysterious Ways

Mimsie Fotheringey was a nasty piece of work.

She had few friends, mostly male hangers-on, interested in her because of her money and glamorous looks, and prepared to indulge her errant personality and unpredictable behaviour. Mimsie was in her early forties and lived alone, except for her serving staff, in a small but lavish country estate near Canterbury in Kent. The estate had been left to Mimsie by her late father, Sir Mark Fotheringey.

Sir Mark made his money in the property boom of the 1980s, and allegedly received his knighthood for services to the construction industry. But there were rumours that he'd donated large sums of money to his favourite political party, and that the knighthood was a favour in return.

Mimsie's mother had divorced Sir Mark, and the girl was spoiled by a father with little idea how to raise a daughter, or the time to spend with her. He took the easy way out and indulged her fondness for expensive playthings, which she discarded when they ceased to amuse her. Mimsie grew up to expect her own way, her face creasing into an ugly pout if she were crossed. Her treatment of men was partly derived from the coldness of her father's behaviour to her, but also from a strong libido. Mimsie loved sex, and especially relished the chase. In this respect, she behaved more like a man than was customary.

She'd started internet dating, because it offered adventures. Besides it was fashionable among her girly set. Bored with the usual club and party scene, they preferred the immediacy offered by the recent influx of dating sites on the web. As long as one had a good sense of judgement, there were some dishy men out there, though there were plenty of duds too.

"You know, internet dating, it's really easy to do it from

home," she informed Vanessa, one of the friends to whom she would boast of her conquests.

"Why hang around the clubs and end up alone at the end of the evening, or with some feeble, pain-in-the-arse wimp? This way is relatively painless."

Mimsie was so attractive that even the most eligible men might hesitate to approach her for fear of rejection. But she also had a reputation for having a scathing mouth on her and a castrating stare. If she took an instant dislike to you, forget it.

"You can't afford me, after all, Peter," said Mimsie, as she delicately swung her expensive-looking legs-to-die-for from her seat, and rose from the table at Posillipo's, a fashionable Italian restaurant in Canterbury. They had dined there one Friday evening in early May. It happened to be soon after parts of Kent were rocked by an earthquake, which had originated in the English Channel.

Some called it an act of God, claiming that the moral fibre of the nation had gone to the dogs, and that the quake was a warning from on high.

Mimsie rubbished this view. She declared herself an atheist, though she'd never really thought through her attitudes to God and religion. Atheism was more a fad with her, and something she used as a means of attracting controversy, which she loved to do. But she'd met a well-known atheist professor at a party, had a brief but passionate fling, and from that time, under his influence, poured scorn on religion. One thing in particular stuck in her throat. She could not understand how any god worth her time, would allow the deaths of the young and innocent. Some David Attenborough story about the diseased kids he'd seen in India, with worms coming from their eyes. That finally put paid to the god thing for Mimsie.

"So Peterkins, I don't plan to meet you again. I really see no point. You look the part alright, and your car just about passes muster, but the reality is that after a couple of months dating you, our suppers together, and regular trysts in bed, I can see more clearly now that you've been stretching yourself just to be in my company. I saw your reaction when the bill for dinner arrived. You looked a most unhappy bunny. And scrutinising the bill like that, as if you half expected me to chip in, I've no doubt that you find it difficult coping with my high maintenance needs. And to tell the truth, your performance in the sack leaves a lot to be desired."

She saw Peter turn pale at her hostility and her utter disregard for propriety, for her words were spoken contemptuously, and in front of the waiter who'd arrived and stood at their table, making ready to process Peter's visa card. He obviously heard what she was saying, for he could be seen to suppress a supercilious look. Mimsie, typical of her, had humiliated Peter, who regularly ate his supper at Posillipo's. Mimsie was sure he wouldn't feel like dining there again. She also knew that he hated her calling him Peterkins, precisely why she called him so.

I don't think Peterkins likes me much. Poor Peterkins.

Nevertheless, he kept his cool, collected his raincoat, and escorted Mimsie to her silver Mercedes. He was on the point of turning away, when she grabbed him and subjected him to a most appalling assault. At first it was a smoochy farewell kiss, for Mimsie needed to know that Peter still fancied her.

"So, Peterkins," she cooed, "one final goodbye kiss."

She was like that, unpredictable. One moment humiliating him in the restaurant, the next, erotically charged, as she leaned into him and flicked out her tongue to open his lips.

Suddenly she bit hard into his tongue, drawing blood. He screamed in pain and prised himself away.

"My God!" he shouted, blood dripping down his chin. "What is it with you? What a piece of work you are!"

9

"God doesn't come into it," she replied. "You know I don't believe in God. You annoyed me back there. You take me for a meal, then look as if you resent paying the bill. Even if you can't really afford it, you should just be dignified about it and pay up without question. That's what a gentleman would do."

She watched him as he turned away, striding off towards his dark blue Fiat Coupe. She wouldn't see him again. She could barely contain a smirk as she watched him, his white mackintosh flapping in the wind.

How flashy he could look.

The day before the Italian restaurant, they'd both received cards notifying them of the tragic demise of a mutual friend, the MP for Hampstead, Algernon Cliff, who'd perished in a pile-up on the M4.

"I shan't attend, I wouldn't be seen dead inside a church!" Mimsie told Peter at Posillipo's, as she drank from her second glass of Châteauneuf-du-Pape '67.

"You know I think all this religious guff is just fairy stories. I am an atheist and that's all there is to it. Anyway, I have an appointment with the architect, David Watt, in Canterbury," she continued. "Our meeting happens to be on the same day as poor Algie's funeral, so you won't see me there. I recently bought a plot of land near Wickhambreaux and have arranged to meet David to discuss his proposals for the house I'm planning to build. Even more exciting, I've fixed up to meet a scrummy-looking man I chat to on the internet. We've met already, and this will be the third time. He's booked a room for us at the Marquis Hotel in Alkham!"

Mimsie had met Peter through an internet dating site, and recounting this new assignation, was a further attempt to humiliate him, culminating in the tongue-biting incident.

Mimsie never dumped one lover, before she'd lined up another. The sadistic behaviour towards Peter was typical of her treatment of men. Like the toys of her girlhood, men were disposable. "Use them, then lose them" was her motto.

Her meeting with the architect put her in a good mood. The plans for Mimsie's new house were exciting. It would be a modern space, open-planned and full of light, with interesting contrasts between curved and straight lines in the design of the interior. There would be imaginative use of local stone, metal, glass, and expensive timber in the construction. She'd have fun selecting the fittings and furniture and would pick the brains of some of her fashionable acquaintances.

She left David Watt's office, full of anticipation. The day was going well, and she felt a tingle as she imagined the promise of the night at the Marquis.

Mimsie slipped into the Mercedes and started the engine. She'd only recently bought the vehicle and still wasn't sure how some things worked. The satnav instruction book was in the glove compartment, but she'd never bothered to read it. She simply followed the procedure shown her when she test drove the car, and pressed a few buttons to programme the directions to Alkham Valley Road, the location of Marquis Hotel.

A gentle rain had started as she swung round from outside the architect's office and set off towards the A2, going south in the direction of Dover and Folkestone. It was already dusk, and she was conscious of needing to drive quickly, to ensure arriving early at the hotel, so she could have a hot bath and pamper herself for the erotic evening in her fantasy.

The rain soon became a downpour and Mimsie increased

the speed of her windscreen wipers. A warm blast from the car heater blew into her face, disturbing her elegantly-coiffured hairstyle. The heater system hadn't worked since soon after the car had been delivered. Something was sticking, and she couldn't switch it off, nor move the dial round to blow air onto the windscreen.

How did the damned thing work? Why didn't she report the fault and make sure the car dealer booked it in for repair?

She poked around a bit, but as hard as she tried, she couldn't get the heater to blow towards the windscreen. The windscreen misted over. Mimsie had to put up with it and occasionally leaned forward and used her gloved hand to clear her vision. It would have to do. She tried to concentrate on following the satnav directions as the rain intensified.

Something familiar caught her attention. She couldn't be sure, but it looked as if a navy-blue car was some distance behind her. Her rear window was clouded over worse than at the front.

Was it Peter's Fiat Coupe?

She didn't think so. She drove on at speed towards the turn off from the A2 to the A260.

Mimsie was not good with technology. She liked to own the latest gadgets; satnav, a top-of-the-range mobile phone, her laptop computer and a recently acquired iPad, but with the exception of the latter, which she constantly used for email and browsing the net, she'd barely familiarised herself with the most basic of their functions. She hoped that the satnav wouldn't steer her in the wrong direction.

"Take the next turning on your right."

Sure enough Suzy was directing her onto the A260. Mimsie liked to humanise her gadgets, giving them girl's names. Her mobile was Marcia, her laptop affectionately dubbed Lucy, and her new iPad had recently been christened Ivy. Mimsie could be such a child.

There was a sudden sharp wind and Mimsie was aware that conditions outside the Mercedes were becoming more hazardous. She slowed down, concerned she might skid on the wet road. She struggled to see in the darkness and had to wipe over the windscreen more frequently. She was perspiring, but couldn't switch off the heater. Her headlights revealed dense woods and slopes to the right of the road. She felt the dampness on her delicate skin. This was not fun. She wished she were safe inside the hotel and hoped Michael would make it all worthwhile. Despite her concern to concentrate on the road, a fantasy about a passionate night with Michael played through her mind like a movie.

The road seemed empty, though she couldn't be sure, as her vision was severely limited. The wind had increased and trees were swaying on either side. Heavy rain splattered into the windscreen. Small branches, twigs and other debris blew across the road and occasionally smashed onto the car. A storm now raged around her and Mimsie knew she was in the wrong place.

It shouldn't be like this.

She hit out at the damned heater. Its blast was unbearable and the sweat poured down her, rivulets of perspiration destroying her make-up, her gloved hands soaking. The steering wheel, like jelly in her hands.

Had she missed the correct turn? Perhaps Suzy's misdirecting her. She really should have read the instructions. Maybe she'd set up the satnav incorrectly.

More dense woods reared up before her as she took a bend. Something darted across the road, and in a moment of fright she slammed on the brakes. Skidding, the car shot

13

across the road, and crashed into a large tree which reared up towards her from the side of a ditch. The vehicle hit the tree trunk, shuddering to rest partly in the ditch. The airbags exploded, inflating instantaneously, and squashing Mimsie's features. She lay there, gasping for air, almost suffocating. She struggled to push away her airbag and managed to prise herself away from its grasp. Fortunately, she was able to raise herself and check her appearance in the vanity mirror. At least her face had been cushioned from serious injury.

Thank God for technology, No, she mustn't invoke God. It's good luck, and modern science that had saved her.

She lay in the car, sprawled across both front seats, feeling sharp pain in her legs and lower back.

A while later she attempted to move and was able to hoist her body into a position where she extracted herself from the seatbelt, and finally cut herself from the air bags. She prised open the door handle.

Making sure she'd taken her shoulder bag, Mimsie struggled from the car and clambered out of the ditch. She felt exhausted and must have looked a wreck. At least she had survived relatively undamaged. She would use her mobile to phone Michael. He would drive out and rescue her. She limped over in the dark to try to find some stable ground where she could compose herself and make the phone call.

This was not to be. Mimsie's luck had run out. Without warning she experienced a falling sensation in the darkness of the wood. She plunged down into some kind of deep hole in the ground. It wasn't a smooth fall. Mimsie was bounced against the sides of a cavern that lay opened up before her, scraping her shoulder and legs against rocky protrusions as she descended.

She crashed onto the cavern floor, screaming in agony.

Mimsie Fotheringey, the once smooth, svelte, fashion plate lady, lay there, a broken doll.

Time passed. Mimsie recovered. She felt around for her bag. She could still phone Michael, anyone, to rescue her. There was no way she could climb out of this pit. She managed to open the bag and feel inside for her mobile. There it was. She touched the button to bring up her contacts and pressed in Michael's name and then his number.

Nothing's happening. It isn't dialling.

She looked at the illuminated face of the mobile.

No signal!

She groaned in frustration and fear. She screamed out in rage. No use. No one to hear her. What was this hell into which she had fallen?

Then it struck her. The recent earthquake. She had read that it had caused serious destruction to property in the Folkestone area. She calculated that she must be a few miles from Folkestone. The Marquis Hotel in Alkham was near the resort, and she'd nearly made it there. Nearly, just wasn't good enough. The earthquake had opened up the land. She'd fallen into a fissure. She recalled hearing that it had been just over four on the Richter scale.

Mimsie lost herself a second time and fell into despair. No signal on her phone. She would die out there in this hell pit. Again, she collapsed into inertia, lying there, cold, soaked and in pain from her injuries, her once beautiful porcelain face bloody, scratched appallingly, cut in places almost to the bone.

She thought she heard a noise. Yes, she was able to make out something, a faint sound. Electronic, a signal? From inside her bag.

Furiously Mimsie gripped her bag and opened the clip

for a second time. She'd returned her mobile to a pocket in her bag, and there it was emitting a glow and a signal. She held it up to her sight. She read out the text message.

> Hello, Mimsie. Please be so good as to read your last email message. I can assure you, it will be your last!

She scrabbled around in the bag for her iPad, and trembling, she switched it on. The illuminated screen cast an eerie glow, which lit her face from below, distorting her normally refined features into an ugly parody. Frantically she tapped the mail icon on the display, held the device in landscape position, feverishly scanned her messages, touched the most recent, and there to her horror and disbelief, she read a sentence which chilled her to the core. The words, in deepest black capital letters, shrieked out to her from Ivy's illuminated screen.

I AM THE LORD YOUR GOD AND I WORK IN MYSTERIOUS WAYS!

A short distance along the road from her pit grave, a man in a white trench coat, switched off his torch, opened the door of his dark blue Coupe, positioned himself calmly in the driver's seat, started the ignition, and drove slowly into the dark.

Johnny Lucifer

Johnny Lucifer was really fed up. He'd had enough. This conspiracy about him had to be stopped. He needed advice about how best to handle his unsatisfactory situation, and so he had finally admitted his true identity to his friend, Arnold Burton, and Arnie, had at least believed him, whereas nobody else would.

"So, you really are the devil," Arnie said, when Johnny showed him the mark behind his ear.

"It's beyond me how you have managed to keep it from me for all these years. I guess that with a surname like yours, 'Lucifer', well, I did sometimes wonder if there might be some kind of connection between you and Old Nick."

"Please don't refer to me by that name," Johnny Lucifer had replied. "And please don't used any of the other names I've been called throughout history. Okay? I don't want to hear anyone ever again call me Satan, or Azazel or Baphomet, or Beelzebub, or Belial or Mastema, or Old Nick, Old Hob or Old Scratch. And definitely not The Prince of Darkness. Get me?"

"Were you really called all those other names? How did that come about?"

"Oh, it's to do with all those crazy religions that people have dreamed up over the centuries. I reckon it was mainly through fear that tribes across the world practised their different religions with explanations for why life existed, who'd put humankind on the planet in the first place, and who was the cause of all the evil in the world. So, they invented me, the devil, or what they thought was me, and put the blame for all the bad stuff on my shoulders. Various tribes came up with different names for me. Something like that anyway. But I don't like any of the other names. Much prefer my own, 'Lucifer'. It means 'light', you know?"

17

Arnie looked at him. They'd known each other for around seven hundred years.

"Of course I know that. What do you take me for?"

"The thing is," continued Johnny, watching that movie, *Angel Heart*, on the telly, has convinced me that I really must do something about my predicament. You know, it's difficult enough being a vampire, and living amongst ordinary mortals, having to put up with all this hostility against our kind over the years, but to have people get it all wrong about me and God, is getting more ridiculous by the day. I mean, we live in an age of so-called enlightened thinking, and it's just not fair that so many people have got the story of me and God the wrong way round. And, they still haven't realised that the beings they call the devil, and all the other demons and angels, are really vampires."

"Well," said Arnie, "now that I know who you really are, I guess I can appreciate why you are depressed about it. And to think that for all these years I just thought we were special because we are both vampires."

"Yes, but you may remember that you only got to be a vampire because I turned you."

"It was such a long time ago," replied, Arnie, "I'd almost forgotten being bitten. But thanks again, my friend. I, for one, like being immortal now, even though for some reason, human blood doesn't seem to taste as good as it used to. Must be all the junk food they eat these days! You are right to feel miffed after watching *Angel Heart*. You're nothing like the devil as Robert de Niro portrayed him in the movie."

"You're telling me! They made De Niro play me all sinister and evil, really creepy. And that silly pretentious name they gave him, 'Louis Cyphre', an appalling corruption of my beautiful name. You know, to rephrase some of the words from that song, 'Maria', from *West Side*

Story, if you say my name 'Lucifer', out loud, 'it's almost like praying'. Don't you think?"

"Yes, it's a great name, 'Johnny Lucifer', I don't know about praying though. I think it's cool and sexy. You are lucky to have such a name."

"Anyway, the other thing they have wrong, is about vampires drinking blood. Don't they realise by now that we only take the blood of wicked people. We never touch the good ones. And when we drink their blood, we turn them, which means they not only become immortal, like I made you, but they stop their evil ways and turn to the path of goodness. Which is what you've done, Arnie. You used to be a thief. Now you are the member of Parliament for Hampstead. I tell you, Arnie, someday people like us will have to rewrite history cos these idiots have it all wrong. Anyway, after seeing that movie I really have to think about how I can begin to change the prevailing ideas concerning the devil and God."

A few days later, and Johnny had seen something on the television news he thought might give him the answer to his problems about being both feared, and terribly unpopular, because he was feared. He marvelled that there were individuals who inspired fear, but despite that, seemed to grip the popular imagination and were held in some kind of weird admiration. People like the boxer Mike Tyson or the ex-footballer turned film star, Vinnie Jones. Few people would want to mess with either of them, yet they were popular in a strange kind of way. The devil was much maligned, feared and certainly not popular, which is why Johnny Lucifer no longer appeared in public, red skinned, with long swishing tail and horns either side of his head. But although his popularity ratings were clearly in decline, God was still highly regarded by a significant number of the population. Up there among the gods. So to speak!

"Mind you," Johnny remarked to Arnie, "this whole Catholic Church paedophile business isn't doing them any favours! A report about child abuse and the Catholic Church had featured on the same news programme and was the other item that had just made him sit up and take notice."

"True," replied Arnie, "but God is still really popular amongst many of the elderly, the poor and downtrodden, and the illiterate, especially in third-world countries. And as for all those fundamentalists. Well, I ask you, blowing themselves up and taking lots of innocent people with them because they think they will end up in heaven, surrounded by virgins. They have it all wrong there. In the first place, there isn't any heaven, as they conceive it, and in the second place, virgins are rubbish at sex. Give me an older, experienced woman any time. So, tell me what did you see on telly that you think might be helpful in improving your image?"

"Well, I will tell you," replied the devil. He was dressed as Johnny Lucifer on that day in early Spring, in a casual pinkish jacket, light blue cotton trousers, deep green sweatshirt and white trainers. He looked relaxed, and there was no sign of a tail or horns. "After the revelations on TV about the Catholic Church, they had an item on this publicist guy, Barry Spinner, a really smooth customer, who seems amazingly effective in promoting his clients. He's been around for a number of years, gets a lot of flak from certain quarters for taking nobodies and making them into somebodies. But he does seem to have a social conscience, and sometimes helps the disadvantaged to turn their stories into success. He also gives a lot to charity. Apparently, he does a bundle of fundraising and media work for the NSPCC. He also helps to raise money for Haven, a school for children with special educational needs."

"Isn't he the guy who represented that footballer who is

supposed to have married an alien?" Arnie said. "He got the story in the popular press, I believe."

"That's him. What do you think? If he takes me on, I reckon he will be able to work out ways to change public opinion. I just hope he isn't a religious nut. It's really important for me to tell it like it is about God and me. It's about time people realised that God is the bad guy and I'm the good guy. Let's face it, you know me well and appreciate that I am, and have always been, a force for good, and let me remind you that 'Lucifer' means 'light-bringer'."

"Sure, I know that, after all, look at all the bad guys you've turned, over the centuries. The world is a far better place since you bit them, and drank their blood. Then they behaved themselves. The more people you turn, the more the world improves. I think you should arrange to see this guy, Spinner, and get a campaign going to reinstate you as the true bringer of light."

So Johnny Lucifer contacted Barry Spinner's office to arrange a meeting. On the phone to Spinner, he had jumped in the deep end and, owned up to being the one and only Devil – the real deal – and that he could prove it. He had intimated that he had a most unusual request.

The following afternoon, he sat opposite the publicist. Then began a conversation which was to lead to events that would fundamentally change the public understanding of God and the devil.

"So, Mr Spinner, let me show you." Johnny turned his head towards the publicist and asked him to look closely at the three numbers hidden under his hair at the nape of the neck.

"I am who I say I am. Please believe me."

Johnny was well aware of the power of money, and that

Spinner believed a liaison with the devil could be a real earner.

There was something really powerful and charismatic about Johnny, something in his feline movements and puckish grin that was slightly devilish. So, he exhibited one of his tricks to reinforce his appeal, emitting a faint luminescence.

"You do know that I am presenting you with an opportunity, don't you?"

Spinner nodded. "Call me Baz." He wore a light grey suit, white shirt and a tan. His head was shaved, and he wore a small silver stud in his left ear. He looked what he was: a confident man, wealthy and debonair, hip and cool. A modern man, in touch with the streets. He talked the talk and Johnny Lucifer felt increasingly confident that Spinner could walk the walk and help achieve the result he needed. Spinner soon leaned forward and poured each of them a cup of coffee.

"Sugar?"

"No thanks, I'm sweet enough." Another impish grin.

Johnny sat calmly and explained his story. On that day he'd dressed more formally, and his appearance was sleek, and handsome, his jet-black hair slicked down. He wore a smart three-piece suit, (he adored wearing waistcoats), a black silk shirt, yellow bow tie, and black patent leather shoes. To be frank, he did indeed look a bit devilish, with a slightly cheeky glint to his eye.

"You may already know some of this, but here goes. God threw me out of Sylvania. That's the dimension where we all lived. It's neither heaven nor hell, though when I was there, I can tell you, he was into making it more like how you people think of the latter. You guys down here really don't have a clue about what exists in parallel with your universe. Please don't laugh. I'm being perfectly serious.

He did this because I had started to question him and was spreading opposition to him among the angels. I was getting the reputation for dissent. It was becoming very political."

"Are you sure that you didn't just resign. That's what I've heard."

"You must appreciate, all this was a long time ago, and there are many different theories about what actually happened. I can guarantee, CallMeBaz, (another puckish grin), that I am telling the truth."

"Well, that isn't the main issue here, whether I believe your story or not. I like your basic idea as you explained it on the phone, and it would be a challenge to promote you in the media. The likelihood that humans have got it all wrong, and that the devil is a good guy. I think the people out there will lap it up. It will sell, and that's the issue here. Besides, I'm an atheist."

Johnny Lucifer continued his explanation.

"The thing is, if you read the Old Testament, you'll appreciate that God is a nasty piece of work, and he was so in my time up there. I just couldn't get on with the guy. He wanted it all his own way."

"So, you just quit, is that it? I thought you said he threw you out?

"Actually, I forced his hand. We had a bust-up over women. We both fancied the same angels. It was getting ridiculous. Every time I chatted up a woman, he butted in and tried to lure her away with his promise of cosmic sex, whatever that is. So I forced a confrontation, and he expelled me from Sylvania, which had become a fascist state, ruled over by that dictator. Naturally I took some of my angels with me, the sexiest women, who also had enough courage to question God's authority. The point is, Baz, I firmly believe that it's noble to explore new ideas and new approaches in the pursuit of truth. I'm the champion of intellect and reason, of liberalism, the open society and critical thinking. I'm the one who stands against the narrow mindedness of God and all stifling orthodoxies. So, are you on my side or what?"

"You know," replied Spinner, "I'm not a money-grabbing, self-seeking smooth operator, although that's what some people think of me. I've even had death threats because I handle some supposedly dodgy characters. I'm a thinking person. I read. I like to study. I must confess that when I read the Old Testament some months ago, I was shocked. You're right, the god in that book demands that we believe everything that he tells us, and that we do everything that he says without questioning."

"Don't you just know it," Lucifer interrupted.

But the publicist was in full flow. He really had the bit between his teeth. He was clearly the right man to champion Johnny Lucifer's cause.

"I think it's in Exodus 5.3, where Moses and Aaron tell the king of Egypt, 'Allow us to travel for three days into the desert to offer sacrifices to the Lord our God. If we don't do so he will kill us with disease or by war.' " He paced around his office, then continued.

"Now I am not an expert on the Bible, and Moses and Aaron may have been trying to bluff the king of Egypt, but this is just one example of control freak God. And let's face it, because the king wouldn't let his chosen people go, God went and slaughtered all the first-born boys in Egypt, young innocent kids, the lot. And he killed all the first-born animals too! I mean, what had they done to deserve this treatment?"

"We obviously share the same attitudes. Let's do some business then. Do you need much time to plan how we can best proceed?"

Johnny Lucifer was trying to control his glowing. "I want to get onto television and tell it like it is. Tell me what ideas would be good for me to do. I can't wait, I really want us to get stuck into this project. I hope you don't think I am rushing you."

"Not at all. There are a number of steps we must take. To some extent it depends on what you are good at, your preferences, how you want to play it. But it could be important to get you to appear on a reality series. That would be a good forum for you to reveal your true self. You must also date a celebrity. We need to keep you in the public eye. Anyone famous you fancy?"

"I fancy lots of them, but Angelina Jolie would be my cup of tea. Not sure if she is with anyone these days." Johnny Lucifer was getting even more excited. Despite his efforts to keep his body in check, his skin was glowing more brightly.

"Turn it down, can you?" the publicist pleaded. "It hurts my eyes. Not sure if Angelina still has the hots for Brad, but don't worry. I can fix it. You will need to do a few photo shoots. Flaunt your body. Is it toned up? Do you work out? Do you still have the tail stump? As long as your body's in good nick…" Johnny Lucifer flinched at that word, "…it'd be good to show it off. The tail stump would really convince them that you are authentic. Can you sing or dance? Maybe we can get you on *Britain's Got Talent* or *The X Factor*. I know Simon."

The office was bathed in Johnny's light, but he'd now made it a soft light, so that Baz would feel more comfortable.

"Sometimes I get my clients to make a home sex video. I don't think that'd be appropriate in this case. Maybe if I can't get Angelina, we can get you to date a member of the Royal Family. On second thoughts that's no good. They are all part of the 'God Squad'. We will set up a website for you, and get you blogging, Set you up on Facebook and YouTube. Once you are better known as the devil, and people feel comfortable with your image, we'll increase our drive to turn you into a popular icon and get your views across on the internet. We can link up with the New Atheists to join with them in spreading the word that it's the devil who is a force for good, and that God is the real problem. What do you think so far, Johnny?"

"Sounds really exciting to me, Baz. I'm so glad I decided to come and see you. Just one thing though. I might as well come clean. You don't know it, but I'm a vampire. Does that change things for you?"

The publicist didn't bat an eyelid. "Heavens no. Oh sorry, Johnny, I shouldn't have used the 'H' word, but anyway, it doesn't change a thing. Actually, I know you. I recognised you the minute you walked into the office. You didn't need to show me the 666 on your neck." The publicist paused, looked directly at Johnny Lucifer, then with a mischievous smile, said, "You really don't know who I am do you?"

Johnny Lucifer looked hard at the publicist.

"It was outside the Candelabra club. You bit me on the neck. You turned me there and then. About ninety years ago it was. I am a vampire too! But enough chat, let's put my plans into practice immediately and go and get that old scoundrel!"

An Apple a Day

Coxes, Golden Delicious, Granny Smiths, Russets, her mum had praised the health-giving properties of the apple ever since Evelyn could remember.

"Keeps the doctor away," chimed her mum most mornings as Eve made ready to leave for school.

And so it seemed to be, for Eve had grown up into a most delightful-looking young woman. Clear porcelain skin, extraordinary red hair, full red lips and a figure to rival Monroe. She was also an expert cook. Her mum, who was a bit old fashioned, had impressed on her that the way to a man's heart was through his stomach. "Some things don't change," she'd told her.

Time passed. School was a memory. At twenty-two, Eve was working as a model with Plus Seven, one of the top London Agencies. Her model book was full of exciting images, from photo shoots, advertising campaigns, magazine features, and stills from video and film work. Monochrome photos of her in sleek and sexy evening gowns, wearing exotic make-up, jostled with full colour action shots, as she ran along a tropical beach, scantily dressed, apparently with little or no make-up, her hair flowing in the breeze; or sportswear pics, taken in a gym flooded with crisp daylight, where she showed the latest line in designer training gear.

Her diet was carefully chosen. In her line of work, she was under pressure to keep her figure in shape, but Eve still ate an apple most mornings, as she was convinced that this fruit, in particular, was good for her appearance and general health.

She had a secret suitor. His name was Adam Wentworth. He was ten years older than her, an account executive in a local advertising agency. They'd first met on a photo shoot.

But the model agency didn't approve of the girls having boyfriends. Adam was tall and muscular with penetrating blue eyes and a silver streak in his jet-black hair. Elvira Hunniford, Plus Seven's owner, had cautioned the new models against boyfriends.

"They will keep you up late, clubbing; and beware those men who want to wine and dine you, and then take you to bed. The wining and dining will make you fat, and the sex may get you pregnant. I cannot have my girls' careers being threatened by such behaviour, so boyfriends are out until you're established in the modelling world, and then we'll see!"

So, Adam was Eve's secret love.

"Let's move in together," he'd suggested, and she'd agreed. And so they found a charming apartment in a smart area, near the centre of the city. Eden Vale was near enough for her to walk in to the agency, and for Adam to cycle to his office, and the apartment was clean and modern, with two bedrooms, bathroom, lounge, good-sized kitchen, and part of a large garden with an apple tree. It was this tree that had clinched the deal for Evelyn. Eve was unaware that Elvira owned an apartment nearby, on the other side of the communal gardens, nor did she know that the agency had accommodation on the estate, which they rented to some of the younger model girls.

"I am sure we will love it here, but Elvira mustn't know," she'd told him. "I can't wait to cook nice things for you. Apple pie would be good. I can pick them from our tree, when the time is right."

She was as good as her word, and in the weeks that followed she revealed her culinary skills, which included recipes featuring apples from their tree. They had apple soufflé, roast chicken and pork with apples, apples in salads, and the most scrumptious apple pies and apple crumble.

For a while, everything was joyous, though Eve had to be careful to keep her relationship a secret from the agency. But time brings changes.

Adam resented not being able to go to some of the places that normally he and Eve would've been able to frequent. The clubs and restaurants where Elvira hung out, were out of bounds. Once they'd discovered that Elvira and some of the models lived nearby, they had to be even more careful. Adam became irritable and began to wish he were free, especially as Eve was needy, craved attention, and was exceedingly jealous if he so much as looked at another girl.

Prior to meeting Eve, Adam had been a womaniser. He was finding it increasingly difficult to repress this aspect of his character. He compared dating women with dining at his favourite restaurants, and maintained the view that one should sample many different dishes.

One Monday morning, Adam left the flat for a meeting to discuss a new account to promote the latest mobile phone from the market leader.

"Adam Wentworth, meet Elvira Hunniford. She runs Plus Seven. We will be casting the models for next week's shoot from her girls."

Adam, looked across at the sultry, tanned blonde, with the delicate red rose tattoo on her left shoulder. It was all he could do to keep his cool. She was stunning, and so obviously attracted to him. Her smile promised everything. He knew, as only a womaniser can, that this creature was going to be a delight. He took her hand and kissed it gallantly.

"A gentleman of the old school I see." Elvira's husky voice made him shiver in sexual anticipation.

"I can be, but then again, I do have another side to me," he teased.

"I can imagine you do. Good to meet you, Adam. I've heard so much about you. Some of it most exciting!" Elvira continued to signal what was on her mind. At that precise moment, it wasn't the advertising campaign.

"Let's talk business, shall we?"

It was Peter Kane, the mobile phone company's marketing man, who'd called the meeting. "That's what we are here for."

For an hour they discussed ideas for the shoot and looked at a number of the model books from Plus Seven. Adam quickly passed over Eve's book.

"I think we need a sleek, futuristic image. Eve is too English country girl, all health and vigour. To me she represents nostalgia, the past. The product is cutting-edge technology, aimed at the fast-moving youth market. We need a girl who looks more rebellious, edgy, even dangerous, don't you think?"

"Sounds good to me," Peter added. "How about Madge Foley, she has an exciting new look. There is an energy to her that most of the girls find hard to produce, and I think she could deliver the sort of challenging looks we've been discussing."

They looked at Madge's portfolio. Decided she was the one they wanted.

"Good," Elvira said and they moved on to select models for supporting roles in the shoot. Peter opened an expensive Champagne.

"A good morning's work demands a celebration." He smiled as he poured the drinks. He called for some trays of finger food, and they relaxed, pleased with their decision.

Elvira made a point of perching herself next to Adam on the black leather couch, while Peter busied himself on the phone. Peter was rarely out of touch with the various departments of his company. With their business concluded, while chatting to whoever was on the other end of the line, he kept his eyes on the passing show of seduction between his two collaborators.

"Pour yourselves more Champagne," he called to them. Adam needed no repeat of this invitation, and filled Elvira's glass, then his own. Peter declined.

So they sat and chatted for another forty-five minutes or so, and Elvira consumed her third glass. Elvira had many qualities, but she could not hold her drink. By the time Peter had poured the last of the second bottle, Elvira was sloshed.

Adam and Elvira, talked incessantly, sharing many interests and experiences. She'd been sitting close to him all this time and touching him on the knee, or the thigh. Occasionally he whispered something to her. Elvira, leaned into him, took his hand and slowly whispered back. "How would you like to meet me soon, for some delicious sex, very soon I hope."

"It's possible," Adam replied. *This woman is a real vixen.*

"Call me at the agency," Elvira said.

The following evening, having phoned Elvira, earlier in the day, Adam began an affair with her. Eve knew nothing. He was able to continue the affair for a while, manipulating his time, so that Eve was kept unaware of his duplicity.

"Terrific apple crumble, Eve." They'd just finished dinner.

"'Fraid I am a trifle tired tonight. Tough day working on some ideas for a pitch we are making for the Genesis account. I am off upstairs to sleep, on my own. I think I'll take the guest bedroom."

Genesis was an American company, specialising in genetically modified foods. Its footprint was international, and despite growing hostility from a public concerned at possible dangers of scientists tinkering with the food chain, it had opened a vast operation in the UK. There was an orchard in

31

the Kent countryside where they grew genetically modified apples. Genesis supplied a chain of supermarkets, one of which had recently opened in the vicinity.

Eve felt a pang of disappointment. She hadn't slept with Adam for over two weeks. He was often tired, or made other excuses. She'd even begun to wonder at his changing attitude to her, for Adam was putting distance between them.
What is going on? she asked herself.
She soon found out.
Adam was normally very careful to cover his tracks, but one time, which was to prove to be calamitous, he screwed up. Eve found the note in his jacket pocket while getting it ready for the dry cleaners.

You are so good in bed... and you know I am too. Kisses. E.

Eve recognised the spidery writing. She threw the note on the floor in shock. She screamed out in rage.
"You rotten pig! You complete piece of rubbish!"
Adam didn't hear this outburst. He wasn't there. He was no doubt in Elvira's bed.

Adam walked back to the apartment flushed from another tryst with Elvira. He stopped at the local Turkish shop.
I'll buy some dates for Eve.
A peace offering. Eve had been miserable of late. No wonder. He'd been virtually ignoring her. He must move out of the apartment, leave her. In the meantime, no reason not to be friendly. He might even get her into the sack again. It would make a change. Adam's appetite had been stimulated by his regular sessions with Elvira, and these days he was invariably horny.
He looked over to the rows of fruit and vegetables. The

store tended to stock what looked like organic produce. Mostly one had to be careful to pick the fruit, avoiding bruised apples or manky-looking oranges. He noticed the rows of apples on wooden trays at the rear of the displays. They were unlike any others he had seen at the shop. They were a beautiful green, clean-looking, pristine, crisp and succulent to the taste he felt sure. Then something happened. He couldn't believe it.

He recoiled in horror. From each apple, all of them, not one left out, there appeared a single white worm crawling from a crack in the shiny skin. Their slimy bodies were almost translucent, Adam could see their insides. They wriggled from the perfect apples. It made him sick. He convulsed and couldn't control the retching, which welled up from his stomach. He gagged over the pavement and down his front. Deniz, the owner, rushed out.

"What's going on? You look terrible. What is the matter? Come let me clean you up." Adam had vomit on his shirt.

"Look at your apples, what's wrong with them?"

The white worms had emerged from their host apples. They'd doubled in size. They were everywhere, crawling over the other fruit and vegetables. Adam and Deniz looked on in horror as the worms slid over the carefully displayed produce, devouring the other fruit and vegetables, until all that was left were the slimy remains.

Deniz rushed inside. He didn't seem to know what to do. He looked for inspiration, something to slaughter these beasts. Then suddenly he grabbed the fire extinguisher, rushed back out and sprayed the foamy substance over the worms. It worked. He didn't know how or why, but the worms were shrivelling, disintegrating into creamy white blobs of goo. They left the appalling mess. Deniz returned inside the shop and poured Adam a cup of herbal tea.

"I don't know about this," Deniz muttered. "People are so keen on the supermarket fruit and veg, and I've been losing business. So I ordered this new produce directly from the wholesale department of Genesis. They assured me the apples were top quality. In fact, they've been selling well. Your lady bought some, a couple of days ago."

Adam eventually made his way home, still shaken, but Deniz had made him shower, and lent him clean clothes.

Eve was all smiles. She was trying harder. She really did seem to believe her mum's advice that the way to a man's heart was through his stomach. She said she wanted him to sample something she'd cooked. She hadn't appreciated that it was not his heart, but another of his organs, that she needed to address more successfully.

"It's a special treat. I've made two really different apple pies, my love."

She poured two glasses of Merlot, and uncovered two pies, which sat on top a cupboard in the kitchen. They looked most appetising, and Adam who felt ravenous after his ordeal, was happy to enter into her little judging contest.

"Taste them both," Eve said. "Tell me which you prefer. One is made with apples from our tree, the other from some I bought locally."

"Not from Deniz, I hope?" Adam recoiled at the thought.

"No, from the supermarket."

"Oh, alright then. That's okay. Let me try a piece."

"Our tree first," said Eve.

Adam tucked into the first pie. It was delicious, but then her pies from their tree always were really tasty. Nothing special here.

"Let's try the second one then. Don't you want any of this?" Adam had noticed that Eve hadn't tasted the first pie.

"I had some before. But I will join you for a piece of this pie."

Eve put the plate with the second apple pie on the table.

34

Adam gazed at it for a while. He felt uneasy for a brief moment. It was much paler in colour than the first one. It was a strange off-white but did look really light and flaky. He felt certain it would have an amazing taste. So he took the slice that Eve handed him.

She ate her own slice, delicately savouring every morsel. They both agreed that this pie was the best. The taste was wonderful. "It takes the biscuit," Adam joked. He felt really sexy, fancied getting Eve to bed.

That evening, in her favourite restaurant, with a group of girls from the agency, Elvira, tucked into her dessert, apple crumble, with cream. It was a lighter colour than she remembered, almost white in fact. But it was really tasty, so she paid no mind to its appearance. Madge Foley ate three slices, two of them, while Elvira had gone to the ladies' room.

A few days passed. Adam and Eve hadn't got out of bed. The post piled up in the hallway, the answer phone crammed with messages.

At Plus Seven, agency staff anxiously awaited some news of Elvira. She hadn't appeared for several days, and what is more, some of the girls hadn't called in either.

"What's happened to them? They all went out to Fangiano's for dinner. Haven't heard a dicky bird from any of them since." This from Julio, the chief booker, on the phone to Peter Kane, who was expecting Elvira and a team of models for the latest shoot. Adam was supposed to be there too. But he hadn't turned up.

Tuesday morning of the next week, there was movement from Adam and Eve's bedroom. They had been in bed for eight days. In her Eden Vale garden pad, Elvira stirred from her bed too. One wouldn't have recognised her, for she was no longer human, although the head was a lightish yellow in colour, and the skin a tawny shade. One might have noticed a red, rose-like marking on the snake's left side.

Rustlings came from Adam and Eve's bedroom. In the half light, filtering from the curtained windows, two entities slithered apart in the bed, pushed their way from under the duvet and glided slowly but purposefully across the bed, curling themselves down to the floor.

In her pad, Elvira, a yellow crowned boa constrictor, crashed from her room and rapidly slid down the stairs. In their rented flats, five of the agency models, the same five who had dined that night with Elvira, the same five who hadn't turned up for work, one by one crawled from their rooms.

As they reached the bottom of the stairs and shimmied across the floor towards the open French windows which led to the garden, Adam, a long, slim, rippling, muscle-bound creature, dark crown with a silver streak, bright blueish snake eyes, entwined himself around a red-topped lithe creature and squeezed her tight in a snakey embrace.

Eve hissed, forked tongue darted from the jaw. Adam recoiled, unwound himself and slid away. He would find Elvira. She would welcome him.

Simultaneously, as if programmed to move out together, the serpents slithered or crashed across their apartments, found openings into the world outside, or if there were none, made them, forcing their way through doors and windows, squeezing through crevices.

And so Adam and Eve, Elvira, Madge, Bettina, Laura, Felicity, and a small rattle snake whose markings bore an uncanny resemblance to the dress worn by Gina the night they all dined at Fangiano's, slithered out into the garden to join the dozens of other serpents: the local residents, who had shopped for their apples at the nearby supermarket.

Dust

David Hetherington made the telephone call he had been contemplating for the last few days.

"Professor Denning, if you please."

He was immediately transferred to Harvey Denning, the eminent chemist and Head of Research at Denning Laboratories, an organisation David had recently funded.

"I will deposit the additional four million into the special account you have established. I am ready for you to work with the new team you have assembled and produce the means for my survival that we have discussed."

David had faith in science, and especially in Professor Harvey Denning. He entertained a revolutionary ambition. He knew enough physics to understand that it was impossible to destroy energy. It intrigued him that when he finally died, his energy would simply take on another form. He would pass on, but into what?

The professor needed no further consultation on a matter that the two of them had been contemplating for the last few months, and which had been the subject of a number of lengthy and intense meetings. The professor had finally convinced his benefactor that he and his colleagues would be able to guarantee that David would live to an age far beyond that of the oldest human ever recorded, given time, and the finance that David, a multi billionaire, could provide. They had met in the professor's office where Denning, an impressive silver-haired figure in his fifties had gone so far as to assure David that he would be able to live a healthy life of at least two hundred years.

"We will not fail in our endeavour. Our research, and the tests you have taken, have identified that you do indeed possess the Methuselah genes, which as I previously explained, have been discovered to enable their carriers a

37

much better chance of living beyond a hundred years, even if they smoke, and consume lots of junk food. We have also found that these genes can delay the processes of age-related illnesses including heart disease and cancer, by up to seventy years. These genes are extremely rare, only one person in a thousand reaches the magic age of one hundred, but you possess the right "suite" of genes to enable you to live well beyond a century."

David's face showed no emotion at this disclosure, for he just knew he was special. He had been tested. He wasn't in the least surprised to be told that he did indeed have the Methuselah genes.

Denning continued, "Our researches have now come to fruition. With some further experimentation I have no doubt that we can provide a programme for you that will grant your wish for a robust, and virile future far beyond any lifespan known to our species. Provided you follow our instructions to the letter, then upon your eventual death, I am confident that we have the means to ensure your rebirth."

David had heard the magic words that he had hoped for. "I am ready when you are," he responded swiftly, bringing the conversation to a close.

It was hard not to be impressed by David Hetherington's tall person, the lean, broad-shouldered frame, handsome face, dark curly hair, distinguished features and piercing blue eyes. As for his intellect: his quick mind and ability to rapidly analyse situations, and come to correct conclusions, helped to ensure him the success in business that had brought him his fortune.

In his personal life, however, it had been a different story. Two failed marriages, several affairs, and innumerable brief encounters with a variety of attractive women, had left him despairing that he would ever find true love, 'the real deal' as he called it. Despite his modern approach to life and his recognition that it was becoming harder to find a woman who would give him more than ninety percent of what he needed in a partner, David still believed in love at first sight, and still craved the one and only woman for him. There was something adolescent, yet almost mystical, in his conviction that somewhere out there was the woman for whom he was intended, if only he could find her. However, his most obvious difficulty was his uncompromising nature, for he sought perfection in his partner. To use the vernacular, she had to tick ALL the boxes!

A couple of months had passed since their phone conversation, and David Hetherington was again in the professor's office at Denning Laboratories, in Kensington.

"We have finally perfected a process which will enable the chemicals that make up your body, to be reconstituted after death, and for you to be reanimated."

Harvey Denning spoke in a most reassuring manner, and David felt confident. He had always felt that he was lucky in his business dealings, and wasn't this just another aspect of his business interests? After all, if it worked for him it could work for other rich people, and vastly increase his fortune!

So, they had found a way of bringing him back from the dead. This was explosive news, and offered the potential to buy him immortality, where he would continue to have the chance to realise his dream of achieving true love.

"You do understand that should your discovery prove valid, you must not share this knowledge until after my death and rebirth?"

No doubt David Hetherington would have then become the richest person in the world, and Denning's team of experts could name their price.

There were many beautiful women keen to meet David. Because of his extreme good looks, virility, and social standing, he still attracted younger women. He was no longer interested in young girls, nor did he fancy older women, mostly because they had aged beyond what he found acceptable. But when he met his dates, he was invariably disappointed, as they never matched up to his ideal. The figure wasn't quite right: a little bit of excess fat here, a bony bit there; or thin lips, dull, lifeless eyes, (he had to have a partner whose eyes sparkled), split ends, rough skin on the elbows, masculine hands, small breasts, big feet. Some had common sounding voices, some smoked, which he hated, others didn't like Italian food which was totally unacceptable to him. How could anyone not like Italian cuisine?

David reached his sixty-fourth birthday. He had been taking the tablets, injecting himself with special drugs, and adopting the other procedures which Harvey Denning had told him would cause the cells of his body to reconstitute soon after death: skin, bone, muscle and hair, all his organs, including heart and brain. He was also assured that his mind would function as effectively as ever, that he would be in full possession of all his faculties, his five senses including his expertise in communicating, his locomotive skills and his memory. He would be alive in all senses of the word. His sex drive would be as strong as before, which was most important, as he had a powerful libido.

But David Hetherington was not one to leave things to chance.

"I need to know that when I eventually die, my decision to have my body cremated will not inhibit the process of bringing me back to life. Can you assure me that cremation will not pose any problems?"

"Believe me, David, there will be no such problems," the professor had replied, and David took him at his word such was his confidence in Denning, and his belief in his own good luck. This was to be their last conversation on this or any other matter.

Sometime earlier, another conversation had taken place between David, and Silas Brunning, a local mortician.

"As I have previously told you, the arrangements I require must be carried out with complete accuracy, the measurements exact, and the front panel and lid of the casket must follow my design to the last detail."

"As you wish, provided that the money is in my company account."

"Don't worry; I have already deposited the 25K. Remember also the special items I need placed inside."

One sunny day, David Hetherington was killed in a car crash. He had signed his will, wherein he had stipulated that his body was to be cremated and to be buried at sea. In his forties he had moved to the Isle of Thanet and lived near the North Foreland shores. A keen swimmer he had become an experienced scuba diver. He felt that burial at sea, with appropriate pomp, would satisfy his fascination with the majesty of oceans, place him close to the scene of some of his most pleasant experiences, and suit his elevated position in society. He had also stipulated other requirements concerning where and how he was to be buried. He left instructions that his resting place was to be between twenty-five and thirty metres deep and ideally off the coast, between Ramsgate to the south and North Foreland, to the north of Broadstairs. There were good reasons why he didn't want to be buried any deeper.

The cremation took place. David's remains were put into a plain urn, carefully placed inside the coffin.

Contrary to popular understanding, the residue after cremation is not ash in the normal sense, but a dusty substance of dried bone fragments, light grey in colour.

A few days after the cremation, the burial at sea took place, on a windy day in July, and the mourners repaired to Mark's home – his eldest son, for a celebration of David's life.

"Why was the coffin so big?" This from David's younger brother Samuel.

"Well, you know David, Mr Big, always had to do things on a large scale," responded David's sister, Lucy.

"Yes, but it also had a really strange-looking lid, with intricate clasp and hinges. Must have cost a small fortune."

It had taken many of the mourners by surprise that the urn containing David's dust, was set into a large coffin-shaped casket, of sufficient dimensions to house a full-sized, somewhat portly human body, with space inside to spare. They hadn't been advised that David had left strict instructions for the casket to be closed, but not sealed too tightly. Had they known this, would they have smelled a rat?

For his part, upon death, David had become energy, and now lay, in the form of greyish dust, inside the urn, which in turn lay within the casket, in thirty metres or so of sea water. Strange as it will seem, inside its repository, the energy was oscillating, the particles of dust bouncing vibrantly. Wave patterns rippled out from the ashes with a vigour denoting a sense of purpose. Dust energy was a living force, had a sense of its own existence, and a confidence about what would come to pass, a zest for life!

The weeks went by.

The casket lay in a stretch of waters at the southern end of the North Sea, off the Thanet coast, near where David Hetherington had lived. Some five thousand years before, this watery grave would have been land, part of a larger coastal region. But the elements had eroded the lands of Thanet, changing its contours, burying evidence of previous settlements, of the bones, muscles, and organs of former inhabitants, other energies, destined to become salt water. The Romans had occupied these lands, from the first century A.D. They had once lived and died there. Perhaps it was the energy of some of their military commanders which washed around the casket as it lay on the seabed. If only the Romans had scientists as advanced as those in David Hetherington's pay, their stories after death might have followed a different pathway.

As the time proceeded, changes had taken place inside the urn and the casket, and were still taking place. They had happened gradually over the months since the casket had sunk to the bottom of the waters. The Head of Research and his team had performed their work with great effect. Professor Harvey Denning had not been joking when he advised David to keep taking the tablets! David was being slowly but inexorably remade. Dust becoming bone, dust becoming human skeleton, dust transforming into organs, muscle, tendon, skin, and hair.

Three months to the day, after the cremation, a light greyish entity burst through its receptacle, smashing the urn to pieces among the plush purple velvet cushioning that lined the inside of the casket. Several weeks later the entity had become flesh, the figure of David Hetherington. In the early morning after the passage of another two days, the figure reached out and located the scuba equipment which had, unknown to his family, been placed to one side of the casket ready for the rebirth.

I have consciousness, I am thinking and I can move. I am alive!

David imagined himself smiling.

I am ready to return to Thanet.

The breathing apparatus would enable him to swim to land, once he had emerged from the casket. But as he lay in the casket and felt his hands, he realised that all was not complete.

My skin it's grey, and too rough, like fine grain sandpaper.

He ran his fingers over the palms. He could feel individual granules. He must wait, perhaps another day or two? He remembered other instructions given to the mortician responsible for placing the urn inside the casket. The scuba was there.

Now where is the rest of my diving outfit, and the other items I demanded?

He reached out and felt under a flap in the velvet lining. Sure enough his fingers grabbed at a wet suit, a mask, and a pair of swim fins. He searched in a pocket at the side of the casket. They were there too, the torch, the mirror, the waterproof watch, and the keys.

But before he tried to put on his wet suit, he wanted to check his appearance. He flicked the switch on the torch. It lit up. His luck had returned to him and once again his luck held.

My skin, it's changing colour.

He could see the skin, rapidly turning, the ash grey becoming his normal skin tone, tanned as he had always been, and finally, smooth. The transformation was complete. It had taken less time for the final stages to happen. He was completely reconstituted as his former self. He strapped the watch onto his left wrist. He clasped the mirror, held it up to his face.

Handsome, really handsome, and younger looking.

This was even better than he had thought possible. The skin was taut and tanned, the hair, thick and jet black, his features regular and still most distinguished. He shone the torch over his torso and felt his body with his free hand. His abdominals, biceps and triceps, solid muscle. His legs felt strong.

He smiled again to himself.

This is just wonderful.

He must reward his scientists when he returned home. He would use his influence to ensure that Professor Harvey Denning received a knighthood. Maybe his luck with women would change, and he would meet someone special, and fall in love. Or was that too much to hope for?

Despite the cramped interior he was able to slide himself into his new attire, and fit the fins onto his feet. He was almost ready to break out of the casket and swim to land. All was proceeding according to his meticulous planning. His foresight and detailed arrangements in the event of an untimely death had ensured nothing was left to chance. His intelligence hadn't deserted him. But what about his returning luck? Good so far, but how would that go now? He was experienced enough in scuba diving to know how to handle the ascent from the casket to the surface, and this was why he had insisted that the casket be buried no more than thirty metres deep, for his scuba training had taught him that this was a reasonable maximum depth for a typical recreational diver. He drew back a moment and carefully donned the mask and put the torch and keys in a large pouch belted onto the wet suit.

And now for the final element in his careful planning. He had conspired with his team to ensure that the design of the casket would feature an escape system, and that this special casket would be delivered to the mortician to house the urn containing his ashes. Confident that he had indeed been interred inside the correct casket, he reached into the top left corner of the coffin to locate a special button.

Good, there it is, ready for me.

David pressed the button, firmly.

My fingers are strong.

He heard a mechanical sound as a motor started up and

activated a mechanism that caused the top of the casket to shoot open with a force that pushed the lid against the pressure from the sea bearing down on the box.

The sea rushed in. But David believed in himself, felt his strength, and forced his way up, out of the casket and into the swirling current. Despite the power of the waters, he kicked out and upwards and soon felt comfortable with the scuba gear. He was able to swim away from the turbulence and slowly upwards, making decompression stops, to avoid getting the bends. It wasn't far to swim to the surface, which is another reason he had chosen this spot.

It was nighttime and he felt cold. He had been in the casket for months and it was winter. But he had succeeded in breaking free from his watery tomb. He took a mobile waterproof satnav device that had been placed in the pouch on his wetsuit, punched in his destination, and was guided westwards towards the Thanet coast, swimming strongly amongst the cold grey waves. He felt no specks of dust irritating him inside the wetsuit, although he believed that any remaining particles would have been washed away by the waters. A strange thought that briefly made him feel uncomfortable, as he didn't relish the idea of losing particles of himself.

The sky appeared a deep blue-black, though the moon cast a highlight on the waves and the water shimmered round him in an eerie glow. All was silent except for the sounds of the sea.

It took him over an hour to reach sight of the beach. He could hear the distant sound of waves crashing against rocks as he swam on. Nearer to the land, he recognised the cliffs at Botany Bay, near Broadstairs, and he swam towards the area of the bay known as the Stacks, huge chalk towers rising up from the sands like giant ghostly sentinels, guarding the main cliffs behind them. The sea became shallow. He checked his watch, nearly two in the morning. The tide was out, and he had to wade knee-deep and then clamber over rocks before he reached the chalk Stacks.

Soon he was on dry land, very cold, hungry, his mouth dry from thirst. He looked around. It appeared deserted.

He removed the heavy scuba equipment and flippers, took a pair of sandals from the pouch, and trudged in over the sand. The colour of the beach reminded him of his own skin tone at the time he had shone the torch on his hands in the final stages of his rebirth and had seen his tan. Had his transformation stabilised? He shone his torch. He had no need to fear. He could see by torch and moonlight that his hands were unchanged, they were still smooth and a tanned colour, though tinged slightly blue from the cold water. He waved the torch around. It illuminated the painted red hut to his right, where the lifeguards hung out in the busy summer season when the beaches were full with local residents and visitors.

Looking up again David realised that he wasn't alone; a young couple had appeared. He needed reassurance and passed closer to them.

"Nice night for a walk, don't you think?"

The couple nodded agreement, the young woman, seemed slightly embarrassed. David wondered what they had been up to at such a late hour. He had visions of certain romantic, if not sexual activities. It had been a long time since he had touched a woman, and he was almost envious.

The young couple seemed unfazed by his appearance. The woman smiled at him.

She smiled, I look normal, she probably thinks I'm an attractive older man. David Hetherington hadn't lost his huge ego.

It's all working!

The young couple walked on and soon disappeared behind the Stacks.

It wasn't easy to carry the diving equipment up the stone steps leading to a pathway at the top of the cliffs, but he seemed to have been reborn with the strength of a much younger man. Once he reached the summit, he gave a last lingering gaze out to the sea which had been his home, then walked from the path into the road, and made his way to a garage at the side of a local hotel. He had rented this place as part of his plan. David took out the keys and opened the garage door. Inside he saw the final stage of his planning. A black Land Rover was parked. There was a large bath towel and a change of clothes in the boot. There were also some toiletries, a razor and shaving cream, blankets and a couple of pillows and some packets of biscuits, bars of chocolate, and bottles of water. Finally, there was a jacket and in the inside pocket, a leather wallet with a stack of fifties, twenties and tens, his credit and debit cards, driving licence, motor insurance and other documents. He dumped his diving gear into the car. He was shivering but ravenous, so he wolfed down some biscuits and chocolate, and greedily drank from one of the bottles. He quickly dried himself off and changed into the clean sweatshirt and underpants, trousers, socks and shoes. He pocketed the wallet but left the jacket inside the car. All the clothes were black, his favourite colour. It suited his tanned skin. He had known that he would be under the sea for months and so had commanded his science team to ensure he would have his usual tan when he transformed. He caught himself musing as to how the black clothes would look against his skin, when it had been a light ash grey.

Probably look really elegant.

But then again, ash grey skin wasn't exactly fashionable. Not in London, let alone in Thanet!

David was tired from his ordeal and he decided to sleep through the night in the Land Rover. It wasn't his most comfortable night's sleep, but he had endured worse, cramped up in his casket after he had been reborn. He removed his shoes, kept everything else on, against the cold, folded down the back seats in the car, set down the pillows, and made himself as comfortable as he could under the blankets.

He slept until mid-morning. When he awoke, he was immediately aware that he was hungry and thirsty. He laced up his shoes and walked over to the side of the garage where he located a tap on the wall. He turned it full on, splashed his face in the cold water and shaved. Suddenly he knew that he must eat, and that he wanted to celebrate his rebirth and his homecoming, and in particular, that he needed a woman. He finished with his toiletries, tidied up his sleeping area inside the Land Rover and donned the jacket. David was in familiar territory, so he decided to drive to the Captain Digby, a good quality family pub and restaurant, which stood on the cliff, overlooking the beach at Kingsgate Bay, on the road from Botany Bay towards Broadstairs. The Land Rover started immediately, no problem there. But then again, he was confident that his luck would not desert him.

He drove along the North Foreland. The North Foreland golf course soon appeared on his right and just round a bend in the road he saw his destination on his left, a large greyish stone, crenelated building. He parked in the car park. A sign in bold black capital letters, about two foot high on a white ground, boldly announced the pub's name. He avoided the larger rear entrance, as he wanted to see the view from the other side. So he walked round the building to an area of tables and benches, and stood alone by the railings, looking down onto the sands of Kingsgate Bay.

There were notices warning people to keep off the railings as the cliffs were dangerous. But he looked over

49

them anyway. He loved the beaches around Broadstairs. There were seven of them, sandy beaches. They were one of the reasons why he had chosen to live in the area. Looking back up, his gaze fell onto a larger crenelated building just on the next bend in the road. Kingsgate Castle, now divided into privately owned residences, had been built in 1760 by Henry Fox, the 1st Lord Holland. Whenever he gazed on this building he felt a sense of history. Here was another reason for living in this part of Thanet. The evidence of history, the overwhelming sense he felt of the passage of time, from before the Romans had colonised the area and through to the present. The unfolding of the story.

His obsession with becoming immortal; it wasn't just about staying alive, to indulge himself in more of the things he liked, and to have a better chance of finding his own true love. It also derived from his fascination with the stories of life. He just didn't want to let go. He wanted to be there to see how things worked out in the future, to live forever, to know the answers, the destiny of humanity.

He turned, walked back to the pub, and went through a smaller entrance into the bar. It was midday, and quiet inside the main bar and seating area, not the height of the season by any means. He decided not to have a full lunch in the Cliff Top Restaurant, which was approached up some steps on the other side of the bar, but strode over to the angular mahogany counter and ordered some sandwiches, a bottle of mineral water and his favourite, a double Courvoisier. And then he sat down, by a small round table, on one of the leather tub chairs, and ate and drank.

And then he saw her.

The woman sat in a corner nursing a glass similar to his own. She drank Courvoisier. She looked truly beautiful. He was immediately smitten. He had finished his food, drunk the most of the bottle of water, so he took his brandy and approached the woman.

"Do you mind if I join you?" He knew instinctively that she would not refuse him.

"How charming, by all means, please sit here," she replied. Her voice reminded him of Rickie Lee Jones, his favourite singer, like a little girl, with a slight cold, utterly captivating. She motioned to him to sit next to her, and as she did so her cool green eyes met his.

She is delicious and seems high class, I must take this easy. Perhaps my bad luck in love is about to change for the better.

The woman introduced herself to David and he reciprocated. Her name, Phyllis Tumelly, seemed to him to possess an erotic charge. They talked. Then they talked more. And then they carried on talking. He bought two more large glasses of the brandy. Then they ordered some desserts and had several cups of black coffee to help reduce the effect of the alcohol.

This woman is everything I have ever wanted and needed. If she is good in bed, I will marry her.

It seemed that Phyllis Tumelly had similar feelings, for she leaned closer to him and from time to time brushed his thigh with her slim fingers.

And then a complete surprise. They were discussing science and medicine, which she intimated was a particular interest.

"I have been collaborating with Professor Harvey Denning on his latest book. I have been commissioned to provide some illustrations."

Phyllis Tumelly was a professional photographer and, he had guessed, in her early thirties. But it was the name of the author of the book that took David by surprise. Harvey Denning, as we have seen, was David's Head of Research.

51

A strange coincidence. But he didn't pursue the matter. He had no intention of telling her his recent past. She would never have believed him, and if he told his secret, she would think he was insane. He would certainly frighten her off.

The afternoon passed, and they made arrangements to meet the next day and walk along the cliff top, and then lunch in Broadstairs in an Italian restaurant. Phyllis adored Italian food. So far she was turning out to be near perfect, possibly perfect! Ninety-nine percent, maybe one hundred percent perfect. Ticking all the boxes! David could not believe how his fortune with a woman seemed to be changing. Perhaps it had something to do with dying and then returning to life in a younger body, though he had no idea whatsoever why this should be the case.

Once they had left the Captain Digby, Phyllis in her silver Mercedes, and David in his Land Rover, he drove past Kingsgate Castle and on into Broadstairs, to a local estate agent, and was lucky to be able to rent some stylish premises which were immediately available. His own mansion home on the outskirts of the town was being completely refurbished for his oldest son, and so he was unable to move back home. Besides, he was yet to reappear to his family and explain his reincarnation.

That would be most interesting. How would they react?

That evening he moved into a large apartment, in a development, overlooking Joss Bay. It was a modern version of art deco and had fantastic sea views. His finances had been carefully organised so that despite leaving various substantial sums of money and other assets in his will, there was a bank account set up for which he had committed to memory the necessary codes. Some of his wealth was in this account. There was also paperwork deliberately left for him, in the glove compartment of the Land Rover, which would guarantee him access to a huge fortune that had been carefully excluded from his will and put into a Swiss Bank account in his name. He would be able to draw on these funds.

The following morning, as they walked, David looked closely at his new amour. Her figure seemed perfection and her features were truly gorgeous: full lips, clear green eyes, pale skin, like the finest silk, hair, a light golden hue, cascaded over slim shoulders, full breasted, an angel. Their discussions had confirmed him in his notion that his luck was in, for there was not one of his interests that she didn't share, and with such enthusiasm that David was excited in ways he could not have imagined. He realised he had fallen in love at first sight, and was convinced that he would be in love with this woman forever.

They stopped, near to the Stacks. Was it only two nights since he had transformed, escaped from the coffin and swam ashore? "I need to kiss you. Is that allowed?"

She leaned into him and pressed her mouth against his, opening her lips. He tasted honey.

The couple continued to meet over the following weeks. He was determined not to rush matters, not to make any overt sexual passes until he felt it was appropriate. For the first time in his life he was attempting to control his desires in his respect for this woman. When they had kissed, he could read her body language. It promised delights, but not quite yet.

After one of their afternoon walks along the beach, she invited him to visit her home in the evening, for dinner. David dressed at around six thirty, not only for dinner, but for seduction. He had bought an extensive wardrobe of the finest male fashions, and chose carefully: a dark blue suit in silk, a navy-blue silk shirt, open at the neck, black patent leather shoes. He wore no jewellery, except a set of solid gold cufflinks, one in the shape of a coffin, the other was urn shaped. No doubt Phyllis would ask, and he would reply that they were to commemorate his dear mother's departing. He would say that she had been cremated and buried in a casket at sea. But the truth was, that in his vanity, he had the cufflinks specially made, only the other day, to remind him of his triumph, thirty metres deep.

Although it wasn't yet summer, the evening was unusually warm and humid as he drove to the house and rang the bell. His hostess soon appeared at the front door. She wore a flimsy silver gown with a plunging neckline. At the back, the garment fell away even more deeply, from her alabaster shoulders, down to just above her waist. She looked stunning. He smiled to himself in anticipation of the night ahead.

Phyllis Tumelly had arranged for the meal to be served in the dining room by extra staff, specially hired for the occasion. Soft music played and low lighting cast a golden glow over the room. The air conditioning kept the room cool, though occasionally they could feel a slight breeze on their bodies. David felt hot with passion. He could read the signs. She was ready for him. This night they would consummate their love.

Over dinner, the conversation was pleasant and easy. Books they both liked, films they wanted to see, musicians and music they admired. He promised to take her to London to see some of the Shakespeare season at the National Theatre. They both shared a love for the theatre. Yet another interest they had in common.

The dinner over, and most of the staff dismissed, the couple retired to the lounge where they sat back on a soft leather sofa and drank more champagne and listened to Rachmaninov from a CD player. For some unknown reason, the air conditioning suddenly developed a fault and stopped working, so Phyllis called in the two servants who had remained in the house and instructed them to arrange a number of electric fans which they carefully placed around the perimeter of the room before departing. The breeze from the fans just reached the sofa and gave a pleasant sensation. The music had stopped, and they sat quietly for a while, sipping at their drinks. Then, when he judged the moment to be appropriate, he leaned towards her and brushed her hair with the tips of his fingers. The woman moved closer to him and ran her hand over his face, delicately stroking his cheek. He took her to him and kissed her softly. He had removed his jacket and so she was able to open more of the buttons of his shirt and stroke his chest.

She squeezed him passionately and opened her mouth fully. Their tongues met, and as they did, her gown slipped from her shoulders, and her warm body pressed against David's naked chest. Her left hand moved down to his thighs.

He looked at her hand, startled. A light grey pallor was creeping over the fingers, and the skin of the hand appeared to be flaking. A slight scratching sound drew his attention to her other hand resting on his shoulder, the fingers were sliding down, the nails had thinned to slivers, scratching the fabric of his shirt as her fingers failed to maintain their grip on him. He saw the hand, dusty and slowly withering, the fingers thinning out, the nails crumbling.

Phyllis leant back and took him into her gaze. She gasped aloud. His face, it was no longer the same tanned colour. A hint of grey had appeared, especially on his lips which she had just kissed. They were the colour of ash. They were slowly decaying. He felt the changes to himself before he saw them. He ran his tongue over his lips. Tongue and lips felt dusty. Dust sprinkled, like bits of dandruff, from his head onto his knees. His shirt was suddenly hanging from him, his shoulders had thinned, his chest collapsing in on itself.

And then the changing gained pace. David saw her shoulders disintegrating into dust while his chest was a cavity covered in fine grey particles. He could no longer hold her tight. His arms and hands were fragmenting into the dust, his dust and hers. His torso was sliding down into the sofa. Her face was slowly caving in. The cheeks two hollows of ash grey.

And then he remembered. "You knew Professor Harvey Denning." David Hetherington could still talk. But only just. "What was he to you? What did he do for you?"

The woman's voice croaked out. "The same as he did for you it seems."

And then they were no longer able to kiss, no longer able to talk, no longer able to touch each other. Phyllis Tumelly had lost her face. It lay, a pile of dust on the leather sofa, like cigarette ash from a hundred ash trays tipped over the leather cushions. The remains of her body, a pile of greying matter falling down onto the floor. Small particles of dust, like sand blown from the beaches, were being dispersed over the room by the breeze from the electric fans. David had flaked into dust, spread out in piles on the sofa and on the floor. As the fans revolved, their breeze blew some of his remains from the sofa onto the carpet, mixing up their dust. Soon it was impossible to tell the dust of David from that of his love. Two glasses of champagne stood unfinished on the leather-topped table in front of the sofa. Filaments of grey matter floated around in their abandoned drinks. Grey mixing with pale gold. Clothes lay strewn around, covered in ash.

As it is said, *what goes around comes around*. David's luck in matters of love, which he thought had finally come up trumps, had gone bust. David and the Phyllis lay in piles of fine greyish granules, on the floor, on the sofa, on their clothing, and spread over the room, lightly dusting the walls, the curtains, the furniture, their particles mixed in together in some places, but separated in others, united, yet divided in powdery grey matter.

The following morning the daily help let herself into the house to commence cleaning the premises. She opened the door into the lounge and immediately saw a silver evening dress, stockings, underwear, high heeled shoes, and some men's clothing and shoes, spread over the sofa and the floor. She bent down and picked up an unusual set of gold cufflinks, in shape, a coffin and an urn. She took a deep breath, blew the dust from them, and put them in her apron pocket. She was taken aback to see the piles of grey dust, and the light coating of ash on the furnishings, so she quickly went to the utility room, took a broom, dustpan and brush, and a large green plastic bucket into the lounge and swept up the mess.

When the cleaning lady had finished, and the remains of David Hetherington and Phyllis Tumelly had been gathered up, several dustpans' full, it might be thought that David's luck hadn't run out on him after all. For it could be seen that most of the loving couple's chemical compounds were at last lying together, in the green plastic bucket.

Tongue Twister

Charles Fortescue was in a most excellent frame of mind. His wife Amy had recently given birth to a delightful baby boy.

"We will name him Douglas Shakespeare, in honour of the great bard," he declared. Typically, Amy played no part in the decision.

But there was another reason why he had wanted to use the name Shakespeare. This was because the playwright was alleged to have command of more words in the English language than anyone else, and because Charles had devised a most radical and ambitious project for his newly-born child.

The bard's vocabulary, as extracted from his works, was over seventeen thousand words, and in some quarters he was regarded to have used around thirty thousand words, twice or even triple the vocabulary of Milton.

"Did you know that Shakespeare introduced between seventeen hundred and three thousand new words into the English vocabulary?" Charles asked his wife.

"Of course not. Why would you know these things?" Charles muttered under his breath as Amy left the room.

During his wife's pregnancy, Charles Fortescue, determined to find the most suitable name for the son he was convinced would be born, had spent time researching the bard. Amy wasn't involved in this pursuit.

Charles was not a literary man. His vocation was science, and especially computer science, and he had designed some of the epoch-making computer chips, which entrepreneurs were profiting from at the time.

Fortescue's processors and other specialised chips, were to be found in some of the world's most sophisticated computer systems. For he had perfected methods of producing a number of the tiniest devices on the planet, devices the size of a micron which is one thousand times smaller than a millimetre, but which enabled the storage, organisation, retrieval and transmission of previously unheard-of amounts of data.

But the scientist had conceived a new project which had originally been inspired by the huge vocabulary of the legendary Shakespeare. Fortescue's driving ambition had initially been to ensure that his child developed the largest vocabulary, and the most extensive command of the languages of the world ever known. But as his ideas developed, he became convinced that he could use his latest chip design to ensure that his son became the most knowledgeable individual on the planet. To that end, he had engaged the services of a surgeon whose specialism was implanting devices into the organs of his subjects.

The surgeon he recruited for his project, Sir Hugo Wilson, worked regularly for international counter espionage authorities, and had been commissioned to implant various tiny devices into different body parts of selected operatives in the service of MI5, MI6, and other important agencies with a pressing need for sensitive information. This business had expanded substantially since 9/11. There were an increasing number of men and women, employed mainly by intelligence agencies, walking around with tracking devices, tiny cameras and sound recorders embedded somewhere on their person. This was valuable business and Wilson was paid handsomely for his work. He had also been knighted for his services towards enhancing the security of the United Kingdom, for with the growth of international terrorism, the times were thought to be more dangerous than in the height of the cold war.

Soon after the birth of his son, Charles met with Sir Hugo.

"I call it Supermind. It's a remarkable piece of technology, and I want you to implant the device inside my son's mouth."

"Supermind consists of a number of tiny chips arranged in rows. They are larger than micron-sized chips, but tiny enough for a number of them to be arranged onto a board smaller than a thumbnail. Look, here it is," the scientist pointed to a tiny object.

Sir Hugo looked on with a degree of fascination.

"Tell me more of what it can do."

"The total amount of information that can be stored on Supermind amounts to one petabyte, or a thousand terabytes. To give you an idea of the extent of this information storage, I can tell you that all the books in The United States Library of Congress, which has over twenty million catalogued books, can be digitised and stored as plain text on twenty terabytes. So Supermind will enable the contents of fifty entire Libraries of Congress to be stored on a chip the size of a fingernail!"

"So, what will be its purpose? Why do you want me to insert Supermind into your boy's mouth?"

"Of course, let me tell you my plans," Charles continued.

"As the boy grows up and develops his skills of speech and writing, the device will perform a number of inter-related functions recording the child's developing vocabulary and speech. Every word, every sentence he utters will be stored. Supermind will classify all aspects of my son's language, and analyse the boy's use of his mother tongue."

He continued his explanation. "But my invention is designed to do much more. I have programmed Supermind with the vocabularies of the world's major tongues, so that

60

over time my son will be taught all the words in all the main languages on the planet. Supermind has also been designed to function as an interactive university. What do you say to me now? Will you perform the surgery I require? You will be handsomely rewarded."

In preliminary discussion about the project, a sum of £75,000 had been mentioned. Working together, the scientist and the surgeon had discussed creating a link between Supermind and young Douglas's brain. The system would then enable interaction between the boy's brain and his developing proficiency with languages, and would automatically filter information into the boy's mind which would be stored. When Douglas thought a question, the device would answer. The father would see to it that his son spent hour upon hour, day after day, having lessons, asking and answering questions, being taught by Supermind. He would rapidly acquire new languages and knowledge, learning how to speak and write the languages for different purposes, for example, speaking or writing to persuade others, or writing a novel, or film script. Douglas Shakespeare Fortescue would be able to converse with anyone of any importance, and if necessary, those of little or no importance. He would also be able to write fluently in any of the languages he had learned.

However, in their discussions, there had been a disagreement between Charles and Sir Hugo.

"You are aware of my expertise, and so let me tell you that I am confident that I can insert a chip directly into the boy's brain, without the need to implant into the tongue and connect it up. I think you should develop Supermind to enable such an operation."

But Charles Fortescue argued that the size of Supermind, even though it was tiny, would create problems were it to be implanted directly into the brain. In truth, he wasn't sure, but was determined that young Douglas would be given a device with the most enormous amount of memory. He had another, more persuasive argument to give the surgeon.

"Sir Hugo, I am determined that Douglas will be provided with at least a petabyte of data storage. In fact, I am working on a chip to store a zettabyte, which is 1,180,591,620,717,411,303,414 bytes! In time, I will require you to implant this more powerful chip into young Douglas. There will be a separate payment for this additional surgery. For the present, the petabyte chip will have to suffice."

This indication of further earnings was enough to sway Sir Hugo, and he agreed to perform the implant into the baby's tongue.

Charles Fortescue had been obsessed with his idea for many years before the boy was born, even before his marriage to Amy. It had taken hold in his imagination and he would hear no objections from her, or from Sir Hugo. He had sworn his wife to secrecy. No one else was to know, at least until the operation had been accomplished and was seen to have been a success. Then, Charles Fortescue had a number of ideas how best to profit from his son's developing and unique abilities.

"I am concerned that your plan, stuffing language and knowledge into the child like that, might damage the boy mentally, and besides it will probably turn him into a freak. I am against it, Charles."

"Don't be so anxious, my dear. I know what I'm doing."

But Amy wasn't reassured but she knew better than to argue with him. Charles was ruthless in pursuit of his goals. He knew she was afraid of triggering his violent temper.

And so, the Supermind chip was implanted into their son, embedded in his tongue, and linked to his brain and

Charles Fortescue set about the task of monitoring the boy's development.

The baby lay in his cot. He was surrounded with large, coloured cards on which could be seen the letters of the alphabet. The sides of the cot had been decorated with a variety of words including 'Mummy', 'Daddy', 'baby', 'cot', 'blanket', 'book', though there were many other words in large colourful letters. Charles Fortescue would frequently lean over the cot, pick up his son, hold him close and speak the letters and the words to his child in a sing-song voice. Within days, Supermind had begun to function as the scientist had planned, and the boy was soon gurgling the sounds of the letters and a few of the words. Normally, a child tries to say words by the age of twelve to eighteen months. Young Douglas, who was already sitting up at four months, was saying some of the words when he was six months old. He had skipped the crawling stage and was walking aged just one year.

A special Scrabble set, with an oversized board and large letters could be seen on the floor in the infant's room that had been equipped with books and various learning aids.

"Come on, Douglas, pick up some letters, that's it. Now make a word on the Scrabble board. What a good boy!"

The infant, now aged a mere two years, was able to choose Scrabble letters and place them on the Scrabble board to form words!

Once a week, Sir Charles would attach probes to the boy which enabled him to download from Supermind, the information about Douglas's language development and ever-expanding knowledge. He engaged the services of specialists to help analyse this material and to publish reports. Charles Fortescue was aware that he was making history, and he wanted it to be accurately recorded.

Most children learn to recognise letters by the ages of three to four. By the age of three, Douglas had an English vocabulary of over five thousand words, which was more than the vocabulary of an average educated conversationalist in the language.

By eight, he had overtaken his famous namesake and had an English vocabulary of over sixty thousand words. By eleven, he had mastered the entire Oxford English Dictionary, about half a million words. He could also speak and write in seventeen languages. He knew many of the Indo-European languages, English, Spanish, Russian, Hindi, French, German, and Italian. He could speak and write some of the Afro-Asiatic tongues including Arabic and Somali. He was skilled in Mandarin, Wu, Thai, and Burmese from the Sino-Tibetan family of languages. He even spoke in Celtic tongues: Scots, Welsh, Irish and Breton.

But Charles carried his son's education much further, wanting to ensure that the boy acquired experience and knowledge far beyond his years. Douglas used Supermind to study the arts, humanities, and sciences. In addition, the boy read prodigiously, watched a multitude of documentary and fiction programmes, and was an avid researcher on the internet. He soaked up information like the proverbial sponge.

"Have you seen *The Wizard of Oz*, Mum? I watched it on DVD yesterday."

"Of course, Douglas. I really love that film."

"Me too, Mum. You know, it was directed by Victor Fleming. He also directed *Gone with the Wind*, for which he won an Academy award for best director. They don't make films like those anymore!"

The strange thing is, Douglas was a lively young man, a lover of films and books, but not a bookworm, as one might have expected him to be. There was only one drawback. Douglas had grown up to be a regular chatterbox. He often gabbled away non-stop. When the boy was in full flight, hardly anyone could get a word in. He could talk the hind leg off an elephant, never mind a donkey! But people put up with it, because he had become so successful in his writing. Aged twelve, Douglas had written six novels, thirty-three short stories, over two hundred poems, and a number of items of non-fiction, including articles on film, photography, football, fishing, and darts. Young Douglas's interests were nothing, if not eclectic.

He had become an international phenomenon. Many of his writings had been published. Two of his novels had been made into films, and he had been interviewed for radio and appeared on television. Douglas was earning a fortune, but because of the boy's tender years, Charles Fortescue looked after the money for him. Given the fact that all this wealth was made possible because of the scientist's invention, he felt entitled to cream-off vast sums for himself and the boy's mother.

Charles was most proud, as well as a lot wealthier, and even his wife was reconciled to her son's achievements and celebrity and had stopped worrying. After all, they now mixed in more exalted circles, and all because of Charles's achievements and the boy's extraordinary abilities with language. It was rumoured in one of the more ridiculous tabloids, that William Shakespeare was turning over in his grave in envy of the young genius.

And then it started.

At first it was gobbledegook words and phrases. Douglas had recently turned thirteen and his parents had thrown a party for him. They had moved into a large mansion in Surrey on the proceeds of the two movies from their son's novels. A number of VIPs had been invited including, the recently elected Prime Minister, Avery Milton, Johnny Wilson the Arsenal goalkeeper and Fenella Martin, the famous BBC news presenter. Douglas was that important. They were invited, they turned up. Of course, there had to be a lot of security about the place. Sir Hugo Wilson, the famous surgeon was also present.

Douglas was to say some words, thanking people for attending. He normally had no trouble speaking in public. In addition to his extraordinary facility with languages, he was physically mature for his years, and self-assured. But Charles and Amy and their guests were totally unprepared for what happened.

The guests had eaten and drunk liberally, and it was time for Douglas to give his prepared speech. Without a hint of nervousness, the boy came forward, and his father called for those assembled to quieten down.

"Thank you all for dimange. It's really groward for you all to be fome. I know that Grood and Fromanger, as well as myself, are triggered to have you all here." He coughed, loudly, then lurched forward in pain.

"Heavens, Douglas, what's the matter?" A concerned Amy rushed forward to her son.

"It's okay, Mum. I'm alright. Please let me finish my welcome speech."

Douglas seemed to have recovered, the coughing had subsided. He wanted to carry on.

"Sorry about that, must be something I ate or drank. Maybe too much red wine!"

The guests laughed. The PM could be heard to remark that the young lad seemed to be quite a card. He for one thought the odd use of language, and what he took to be the fake coughing and spluttering, was all part of a comic act to keep the guests amused.

"Anyway," Douglas continued, "thanks again for triffing it. I am most greetol to Grood and Fromanger, for arranging this driteming. La plume de ma tante est sur le bureau de mon oncle, et vipera est in longa herba. Waldhing fort ynotering stumpinger."

The boy seemed to go into a dizzy spell. Then he made weird body movements, shaking and convulsing as he pronounced the last of these strange words. Finally, he collapsed on the floor. The guests had no idea what was going on, and Douglas's parents rushed forward, and lifting him up, took him from the room, leaving the party to stand there in amazement. The conversation buzzed around, but they had no explanation for what they had just witnessed.

"I think it might be kindest to leave," the PM said, as Charles Fortescue re-entered the room. "I am sure we all hope that the boy recovers from whatever illness came over him just now."

"Yes, yes, Prime Minister. I am sure it's just nerves. Perhaps as Douglas himself indicated before, it's something he has eaten. I really don't know what to say. His mother is with him. I do apologise for the party ending so abruptly."

Soon all the guests had departed, chattering as they left, about the strange behaviour of the young man. In the house, Douglas had gone to bed, though his father was determined to get to talk to him as soon as he had recovered. The boy had been behaving strangely, even before the incident at the party. Charles had noticed that occasionally he did seem to mix up a few words and phrases. He was most determined to find out what had gone wrong.

Surely Douglas wasn't developing an uncooperative streak, deliberately trying to embarrass me, to sabotage all I have worked for?

"Maybe he is going through an adolescent rebellious phase," he commented to Amy.

She simply nodded. She had clearly been against the idea from the start, but had been walked over, as Charles had walked over many others to achieve his position at the top of his profession. Charles felt it was very worrying. The boy had an obligation to continue the good work they had started together. It just wouldn't do for his son to try to back out of this project.

The following day they were both concerned when Douglas didn't emerge for breakfast. They called him down. He didn't come.

"I will go up to his room and see what's the matter. Charles was soon knocking at his son's door.

"Douglas, are you alright?"

No answer.

"Doug? Douglas?"

Still no answer.

For a young man with such a huge vocabulary, and so used to talking incessantly, his son was uncharacteristically subdued.

He knocked on the bedroom door.

"Can I come in?"

No response.

"Douglas, I am going to open the door. I am coming in. I am worried about you."

He waited a while longer, but the boy uttered not one word, not one sound. He pushed open the door and entered his son's room. The room was in shadow. He switched on the light. He looked over to the bed. It was empty. The duvet was on the floor. But he noticed a strange, small, lump shape in the bed, sticking up from under the sheet. There was red staining on the sheet. Charles moved quietly forward, towards the bed.

"Douglas. Are you okay? Where are you?"

He looked in the en suite. Douglas wasn't there.

"Where are you? Hiding from me? What's wrong?"

He darted back towards the bed in a panic. And then noticed the window to the side of the bed. It was open.

Had he gone through the open window?

Douglas was crouching in the garden below, his body bent over, his arms wrapped around his legs. His head bent forward onto his knees, which were drawn up. He was shaking in an exaggerated motion, making strange noises, gurgling noises, loudly as if in extreme pain. Charles could see it. He could hear him. He was concerned.

What was going on? And what was that lump in the bed?

He came away from the window, bent over the bed and gingerly drew back the thin sheet. And lying there, in a small pool of dried blood, a large fleshy object, purple-pink flesh, twisted into a grotesque shape. His tongue.

A week later. In the drawing room of the Fortescue residence. Charles Fortescue has met with Sir Hugo Wilson. They stood by the window, near the ornate velvet-covered sofa and some chairs. Charles had poured two large brandies. The surgeon was speaking.

"I can only give you my guess as to what may have happened to your son. I have examined the lump that you discovered under the bed sheet. It was immediately recognisable as a human tongue. And when you brought in your boy from the garden, he had suffered the most appalling, and agonising trauma. His tongue had come away from the floor of his mouth. It seems to have twisted itself viciously to become detached from its anchorage, the hyoid bone, which as you know, lies under the lower jawbone. It had also twisted away from the muscles at the rear of the mouth, which are themselves attached to an outgrowth at the base of the skull."

Charles took a large gulp from his brandy and gripped the back of the sofa. He didn't say a word.

"When I examined the tongue, I saw that, as well as its twisted shape, it had become swollen to over twice its normal size, and was ridden with strange indentations. Of course, I looked to see if Supermind was still embedded inside the muscle. It was, but it was seriously damaged and had expanded to the point where it was sticking through the surface of the muscle. I also investigated the minute connections I had made from Supermind and up into the unfortunate boy's brain. They had fallen away from their locations and were lying there loose inside the oral cavity."

Charles had still not spoken and remained silent. The surgeon sat down but continued his analysis.

"Now, Charles. I have a partial explanation for this terrifying ordeal your boy has suffered. Clearly our plan has backfired. It has gone horribly wrong. I think that as he developed languages and knowledge at the most rapid rate one could imagine, the memory banks of Supermind malfunctioned. They should have been able to contain the trillions of bytes of information. After all, you designed them to do so. However, I'm afraid that there seems to have been a flaw in the memory systems and the chips have overloaded."

Charles sank down into the sofa, visibly shaken. Sir Hugo swallowed a measure of his drink and continued.

"Also, I think the saliva in the boy's mouth may have caused additional problems. Perhaps there was a chemical reaction which caused a burn out, an electrical shock. Perhaps a number of such catastrophes, which also caused the connections between Supermind and Douglas's brain to become dislodged. From what I witnessed at the boy's thirteenth birthday celebration, your son's behaviour was a warning at that time that something was seriously amiss."

"But how? Why?" muttered Charles. "It was all going so well. Douglas was famous, his books were selling internationally. I am convinced he would have developed language beyond our wildest dreams. Supermind was a mind-boggling achievement. I worked on it for years. It can't just fail!"

"Charles! Listen to you. Not a word of sympathy for your son. He is disfigured. He has no tongue. He cannot talk. He is brain damaged."

"Well, you are the best there is. I am confident that you can put him back together. We will overcome this setback. He will talk again, and write again. More, and even better than before. You can do this for me. I will pay you well."

The surgeon, ignoring his unfinished brandy, rose from his chair, walked over to the door, and took his coat from the coat rack. He turned and addressed Charles.

"I am afraid not. There is little I can do. I could try an operation to attach Douglas's tongue, but I am not sure I could untwist it. Besides, the boy's brain is severely damaged. His mind is shot. He will never speak or write again."

The surgeon departed. He didn't return to reattach the tongue. He never saw Charles or Douglas again.

A House with Character

Emily Mayhew, unmarried, appeared a nervous lady in her forties. Emily seemed uncomfortable when she first met Julian Deans, a local estate agent in his early fifties. She explained that she was a single person looking to buy an apartment in a house with character.

"Edwardian or Victorian, but preferably Edwardian. I love those old, solidly-built houses. They are substantial, and give me a sense of security." Emily explained to the agent that she was assistant librarian at a college in the West End.

"I love my job because I love books and what is more, I delight in being of use in helping young people to gain knowledge and improve themselves."

"What a coincidence. My mum was a librarian," Julian told her. He revealed that he liked to read science fiction.

"What books do you like?"

"My favourite books are crime thrillers, horror stories and fantasy. My sister writes horror stories. She is quite successful."

Julian found Emily Mayhew's taste in literature difficult to credit. It gave the lie to her outward appearance, shy manner and nervous disposition.

Perhaps, in her reading habits, Ms Mayhew could identify with extreme behaviour, which she could never experience in her own existence. And so her reading brought a degree of excitement into an otherwise drab existence.

This was Julian's rationalisation of the woman who'd entered his office. Julian was a bit of an amateur psychologist. Not all estate agents are wide-boy property jocks.

Nothing wrong with a bit of escapism.

72

The odd thing was how easily she confided in him. On her second visit to the agency she told him that she longed for some adventure, perhaps romance with a kind man, or foreign travel. The former was unlikely, though she wasn't unattractive. Despite her small build, washed-out face, pale grey eyes, and old-fashioned hair style, under her clothing Emily had a shapely, voluptuous body and could, with some help in the style department, including the right make-up, have certain types of men lusting after her.

Another of Julian's interests was fashion. He'd studied fashion design but found it almost impossible to make his way in the fashion industry and so ended up in property. But he had an eye for the way people presented themselves.

Julian Deans was surprised, when she called in to his office a third time, to find himself revising his earlier impression of Emily as a plain Jane.

What was it about her?

It was the height of summer, a hot day. She wore a calf-length skirt, made of thin cotton, and a pale blue blouse. Her shoes were functional with a small heel. She'd brushed her hair differently and taken more care with her make-up. The look was bland, yet Julian could see the contours of her figure and was unusually excited.

"I bet she is really sexy underneath, if only one could get her to respond," he'd remarked to a colleague in the office.

"Fat chance of that," replied John Ionnedes, one of the agency's recently-appointed negotiators.

"Is she going to buy that flat? That's what you should be concentrating on. Not getting off on some crazy flight of your fertile imagination. You have no chance with Miss Prim, I cannot imagine her letting a man get anywhere near."

"Hmm. I am not so sure. I admit it would take all of my charm. I might have to court her for weeks, months even, before I got a look in. Still there is something about her, and I might just give it a go."

"Well, I think you would be wasting your time, is what I say."

"And in answer to your question, I am meeting her outside 14 Waverley House later this afternoon. She is going to view flat 2. I hope she takes no notice of all the 'for sale' boards in the front. I don't want her asking the wrong questions. There were five out there the last time I looked. Mike Brimley has given it to multiple agents."

"How long has it been on the market?" Ionnedes asked. "Seven months?"

"And then some," replied Deans. "It's been on our books over a year. When it first came onto the market, it was impossible to keep the history of number 14 Waverley House out of the press. It's only a matter of time before Emily Mayhew discovers its gruesome past. So far she hasn't found out. You may recall she wants to move into the area from south London, as she is about to change jobs. This part of town is unfamiliar to her. Let's hope it stays that way and she buys the damn flat! I will be over the moon to get it off our books, which is one reason we have dropped our commission to half a percent to encourage Brimley to drop the price."

"What was it originally?" asked Ionnedes, "£445k? Not bad for the normal two-bedder around here."

"The point is number 14 isn't normal. Brimley has dropped the price by stages. It's now, as you well know, on the market for £327k, one helluva price drop! I would buy it myself, as a buy-to-let, if I was sure I could rent it out."

"Wise not to take the risk is what I say," Ionnedes replied. "Good luck this afternoon when you meet Miss Prim."

"You know it would be great if I could score on both fronts, sell her that flat, and get a feel of that figure. And then, when she is ready, do the business. I wouldn't try to rush, but I just sense that there is more to this lady than meets the eye. You know, I don't think I told you before, I was raised by women, never saw Dad till I was six. He was abroad, in the army. Think I have a natural intuition about how to play a woman. Besides women really interest me, they are wonderful. Never wanted to settle with one though."

"You are such a male chauvinist. You should be like me, happily married, faithful. Love my wife, adore my kids. You are missing out. All this wasted energy, running around on the chase."

"The chase is my choice, wouldn't want it any other way. Live a bit near the edge, is what I say."

Julian Deans couldn't resist a playful dig at his colleague.

"So, what do you say to that?"

He grinned across the desk.

Julian watched as Ionnedes turned to his computer screen and tapped into the agency website to check out the display on their homepage. It was his responsibility to update the pages. He said he wanted to make sure that a recent addition to their for-sale property portfolio had been uploaded.

Satisfied, he turned back to Julian.

"Did she take away the details of number 14? That's what I say."

"Yep, absolutely. Of course, nothing on the information page to indicate anything untoward about the place. No mention of its former owner before Brimley bought it. Brimley is a weirdo to say the least. He really got off on living there. Some people. It beats me! Don't think I could handle the place. But Brimley fell over himself when it came on the market, paid the full asking. Unbelievable!"

"Well it paid out for him didn't it? He ran those kinky singles parties there. Enough oddballs wanted to breathe in the atmosphere of the place where all those body parts were dug up."

4.00 pm, outside number 14 Waverley House. Julian Deans, waiting for Emily Mayhew. She soon appeared, driving up in her pale green Fiat Punto. *What was it about this woman and her awful colour sense?* As she got out from the car he couldn't help notice her thighs. The skirt was slit at the front, and he got a good look at her legs. His sense of excitement mounted.

How do I play this? Slowly, got to get her confidence. Mustn't come on too quick.

"Hello, Emily, good to see you are on time."

He called her by her first name to try to encourage her to connect more personally with him. Being too formal would never get him what he wanted.

"Julian, nice to see you. Shall we go in? I have seen the front of the house. I drove by earlier."

She seemed surprisingly at ease, unlike the nervous Emily who had walked into his office on the three previous occasions. He noticed the large red leather bag slung over her shoulder, and the stylish designer shoes; Christian Louboutin, he recognised the trademark glossy red soles. He felt immediately that her style was far less restrained than before. The shoes had a higher heel.

More sensual, definitely sultry looking.

They approached the front entrance. The house was Edwardian, and a porch led them to the front door painted a smart navy blue. The owners of the four flats, two up and two downstairs, had clubbed together to try to brighten up the place, and so the entrance hall was painted a summery pale yellow and there was good quality carpet in the common parts. Flat 2, occupying the front half of the ground floor, featured an unusual iron-grey door with brass door furniture.

Julian took his bunch of keys, soon found the right one, and opened the door. Inside, he and Emily surveyed the rooms: a large living room, a dine-in kitchen, two good-sized bedrooms and a main bathroom. The principal bedroom had an en suite. There was a communal garden, but no off-street parking. Emily would have to leave her Punto parked on the road.

Julian decided to try to gain Emily's trust and mention a minor issue with the refurbishment. Emily had noticed that some of the floorboards in the living room and the main bedroom creaked.

"You might have to take them up and start again," he said.

They were standing in the main bedroom. Julian had visions of bedding her there and then. He kept his composure.

"Fine, once the flat is yours you can soon do that. Won't be cheap though."

What he really wanted was to make a pass at this woman, who much more than before, seemed to entice. Her voice had softened, her blouse revealed a distinct cleavage. Julian grew hotter, the flat was stifling. All the windows were closed for obvious security reasons. In direct sunlight, the heat inside made him perspire.

I must keep my mind on the job, and sell this lady, Flat 2 Waverley House.

"So Julian, tell me the history of the house. I hope you don't have to rush off to another appointment. I had wondered if we might get to know each other better. A lot better, possibly."

Heavens, she is coming on to me!

Julian couldn't believe his luck. He mustn't tell her the real story about this house, that would never do.

"The owner, a chap called Brimley, has dropped the price substantially, as you might have discovered." Julian evaded other details.

"I won't pretend. At first Brimley had hoped to beat the market, but prices in the area dropped a bit in line with the market trend, and he has had a change of fortune, needs the money quickly, and so we reduced the price substantially. Emily it's a bargain. Buy it and let's go out this evening to celebrate. Come back to the office and we can get the ball rolling. Perhaps it's unprofessional of me, but I must tell you I fancy you to bits, Emily."

"And I am attracted to you too Julian."

This was better than he could have expected. He would get her back to his place later, he was sure of it.

"But you are not being totally honest with me, Julian. Tell me the history of the flat before Brimley."

"Ermm, not sure what you want to know. I haven't been in this agency very long, so I am not familiar with the details of Waverley House before Brimley moved in. I do believe he had it totally refurbished."

"You are damned right he did," hissed Emily Mayhew, a cold sneer crossing her thin features.

"The garden was an open pit, and the floorboards had all been dug up in here. They've not been replaced too successfully either! As I said, you are holding something back aren't you, Mr Julian Deans?"

Julian Deans was suddenly aware that the atmosphere in the bedroom had changed. Emily Mayhew's demeanour had gone from sweet and enticing to menacing, in the space of a few moments. The sweat was pouring from Julian's brow, and under his arms it was clammy. He was glad to be wearing his business suit, as it hid the damp patches on his shirt, though of course he was warmer in his jacket than was comfortable.

The afternoon sun had faded, and the room was now in half light, but still warm, and he felt claustrophobic. Emily, however, seemed cool, and almost in charge of the proceedings.

"Holding back? What do you mean?"

"Aww come on, Mr Deans, don't try to con a con artist. You really don't know what you are dealing with here."

Emily seemed to grow in stature, and Julian realised that she had drawn herself up to her full height. The high heels made a difference. He was very confused.

How had she managed to appear so demure on her visits to his office?

Suddenly, she raised the tension. She became even more aggressive. Her voice louder.

"Let me tell you about this place? I know its history very well. I lived here you see, at the same time he did. I heard a lot of what he got up to. I mean I could hear him from my upstairs apartment. I heard the sex, the screams, and more. This flat was his, you know. The adjacent downstairs flat was unoccupied, and the owner of the other flat upstairs, was abroad at the time. So there were just two of us living in the house. Me and Joey Dunning. You recall Joey Dunning, don't you? The handsome, enigmatic Joey, the famous television presenter. Had women falling all over him. Little did they know. Then, it was in all the newspapers, and on television. So don't make out you're ignorant of Joey Dunning, serial rapist and murderer!"

Forget about having sex with this woman. There is something wrong with her. Julian now felt that Emily Mayhew was one disturbed lady. He was afraid of what she might do next.

She paced the room. The floorboards creaked; the sound grated in his head. Suddenly she turned. She wielded a large knife in her left hand. She must have hidden it in her shoulder bag.

"Let's cut this nonsense," she rasped. "I'll tell you about this hell-hole and the women he raped, killed and dismembered. There were seven of them. He picked them up from the pub at the top of the hill. Oh, he was a real smooth one, and so good looking. I was pretty glamorous in those days. You wouldn't believe it now though, would you?"

Julian made no reply. She was beside herself, waving the knife around pointing it threateningly at Julian, with sharp stabbing movements. The room had taken on a sinister appearance as the light was fading fast. A pale moon threw a faint, ghostly illumination through the front windows.

"I fell for him myself. I shudder at my own stupidity. He had me here in his bedroom, one Friday night. The weekend stretched before us. I was looking forward to a steamy couple of days, just me and him. Then he went all peculiar on me, started talking mad, about me being just the right size to fit in his wardrobe. He had taken a pair of stockings from a cupboard drawer and was twisting them around and looking at my neck. He was breathing heavily and perspiring. He looked evil."

She was circling Julian, still viciously pointing the knife, clearly on edge. She might snap at any moment. The estate agent would probably be able to overpower her, though he wasn't about to try to tussle with this seemingly half mad creature with the knife.

"Heaven knows what he would have done with me," she rasped. "He had got me drunk you see. I really didn't know what I was doing. I panicked and lashed out at him, but he overpowered me, had me on the floor. He was straddling me. Then I had enormous luck, I still don't know why. But his phone rang, and he just got up and ran from the flat in some kind of panic. I got out of there. I phoned the police. It was me who got them to come over. They searched his place, found items, female things. The following morning, Dunning hadn't returned. The police reappeared this time with sniffer dogs. They dug up the garden and found the remains of seven women. I had heard some of their last moments from my rooms upstairs. Yet I still came down here to be with him. What was wrong with me then? Well, I am fine and dandy now Mr Julian F'ing Dean! Just that I do not know how to behave among men, I cannot trust men, and I cannot trust myself."

She broke down, burst into tears. The woman was struggling with herself.

"Put that knife away, Emily, you know you are not going to use it. Tell me why did you come here. Surely, having gone through what you experienced with Dunning and knowing what you know about this place, you would have kept away?"

Her outburst seemed to have calmed her down. A full minute passed before either of them spoke again. Julian waited, hoping that she would keep herself under control. He looked at her, kindly, hoping that when she met his gaze she would feel reassured.

Emily had returned the knife to her shoulder bag, then finally, with a quiet sobbing voice she answered him.

"Why I came into your office? Why I wanted to see this place? I needed to do something to try to drive the nightmare from me, and so I posed as a prospective buyer. I felt compelled to come here again, to get inside, see how it is now, try to bring it all back. I hoped it might help me to live quietly with myself. You have no idea how much my past has been haunting me, has made me lose my former self. I don't know who I am anymore. Julian, you appear to be a kind person. Can I trust you? Can you help me please?"

Julian didn't know his own thoughts and feelings. He still felt a sexual compulsion for this woman. Of that he was sure. Yet, given her past, of which he was now painfully aware, she could turn out to be a heap of trouble. How was he going to play this one? He didn't know, though he lusted after Emily Mayhew even more.

As they turned towards the front door and made their exit, he took a gamble.

"I have another viewing here this evening. A lady wants to buy a flat in a house with character. I haven't met her yet. The appointment was made on the telephone by my colleague. Then, after the viewing, maybe we can still go out to dine. Strange thing is, she has the same surname as you."

"That would be Alice Mayhew, my twin sister. She was the owner of the other first floor flat, adjacent to mine. We bought at the same time, when the house was first converted into four apartments," Emily said, a strange half smile crossing her face. "She sold her flat and moved to the States. The novelist. You remember I mentioned her, she writes horror stories."

Time Flies

Mickey Abrahams sat dozing in the garden. He was perched closer to the lawn than normal, because he had carried the Shiva chair outside. It is customry in the Jewish faith, after a death in the family, for the mourners to sit on low stools. Although he was only forty-seven, Mickey suffered from back trouble, and rather than sit uncomfortably on a Shiva stool, he'd asked his brother-in-law, Aaron, to saw off some inches from an old family chair. At least he had support for his back. But his problem in the lumbar region wasn't the greatest of his tribulations.

Mickey sat Shiva for six days, since the death of his beloved wife, Esther. There was one more day to complete the cycle. According to Jewish belief, humanity is at the centre of the world, which was created in seven days. When creation is reversed, the soul returns to its origins, and that process is marked with a week, where the immediate family of mourners sit Shiva in the home of the deceased. For the entire week of the Shiva, the family of the deceased remain in the house of mourning, and their relatives, friends and members of the community visit to console the mourners and participate in evening prayers.

Esther was thirty-six when she died. She was beautiful and a good person. Micky adored her. He was devastated to lose her. Esther died of a cerebral aneurism. Over the years, a blood vessel began to bulge and had finally popped, like an over-inflated balloon. This condition is usually asymptomatic, and it was so in Esther's case. It came unannounced, and struck this young, healthy Jewish wife and mother, during a tender moment with her husband. They'd been holding each other, affectionately.

"I am having a really bad headache," she moaned. "It has just started, but it's so intense."

Then suddenly she convulsed and within a few moments was lying comatose in his arms. Nothing could have been more frightening for the husband. Esther died on the way to hospital.

Family and friends suspected that Esther's death was caused by the strain she'd put on herself in her training schedule. For Esther was an experienced marathon and triathlon competitor. She'd run the London Marathon six times, and had competed in numerous triathlons. That same morning, she'd risen early and commenced a gruelling bike ride in preparation for the hundred-kilometre cycle section of the Challenger, the ultimate triathlon, which required eight months of hard training.

Mickey and Esther were the parents of a young son. Eli was five years old at the time of his mother's death. He was initially told that Esther had gone away for a while, as part of her training. But when Mickey realised he would have to explain the Shiva to the boy, he had to tell him that he would not see his mummy until he went to join her in heaven. Eli would have to understand that it would be many years before Eli and Mummy could meet again.

The sun was shining brightly in the garden as Mickey dozed. He started from his sleep, disturbed by the feeling of something brushing against his head. It felt very gentle, and very strange, but at that time, Mickey was extremely stressed, and wasn't quite himself. He was now awake, but still a little drowsy. Perhaps he'd imagined being touched. Maybe a large leaf had fallen from the chestnut tree nearby and wafted down to drift across his hair. He looked around him; he couldn't see any large leaves anywhere.

One more evening of the Shiva. Then I can take down

the covers on the mirrors and get back to wearing proper shoes.

It is traditional to cover over the mirrors and pictures in a house of mourning, from the moment of death until the end of the Shiva. Mourners must also go around in stockinged feet, or wear insubstantial footwear, such as slippers. Both these practices are a symbolic disregard of vanity and comfort, the better to be able to concentrate on the deeper meanings in life.

He noticed how green the grass looked. Mickey had mown the lawn on the day before Esther had died. Now the sun shone through the blades, illuminating them like little filaments of green glass. He estimated that each blade stood between four and six centimetres.

The lawn has grown. I will soon need to mow it once more.

And then, as quickly as he could, given his sore back, he raised himself up from his seat in alarm. He looked at the grass.

Surely not!

Mickey Abrahams sat down again and gripped the arms of the low chair to steady himself. He gazed in wonder at the lawn beneath.

The blades of grass are moving, rising higher by tiny fractions. This is unreal!

He was sure he could see the movement. He concentrated, focussed on the grass. He was nearer to it than would be the case if he were sitting on a chair with normal legs. The fact that the Shiva chair had its legs sawn short, wasn't the issue. The grass was growing more quickly than it should. It was as if he were watching a time-lapse film sequence, where time has been speeded up. He was sure the sky had darkened a little.

Maybe it was going to rain.

Mickey pinched himself. He was awake, not in a dream. He recalled the odd sensation of waking up with the feeling that his head had just been touched. His imagination ran riot.

Was the movement of the grass related in some way? That's ridiculous!

When he looked down again at the lawn, he couldn't believe his eyes. The growth of the blades seemed to be speeding up. He could see it more clearly. The blades were at least three centimetres longer than when he first noticed the change. He raised himself from the Shiva chair, his back giving him grief. But he wanted to bend down more closely to examine the grass.

On his hands and knees Mickey moved himself close towards the blades of translucent green. He looked, concentrating. All his effort focussing on the separate grass fibres. He saw them individually, sharp, pristine, bright. The blades were stretching upwards, reaching out to his face, growing even more rapidly than before. Some of them were almost touching the tip of his nose. And then they were caressing him. He felt the softness as they wafted in the breeze against his features. It felt delightful. It was also impossible!

Mickey pinched himself again, like Alice in Wonderland. But it made no difference. This was real. He was in his garden, his beautiful Esther had passed on over a week ago, and there he was, convinced that he was witnessing the grass growing, twenty times, maybe fifty times, maybe a hundred times faster than normal.

This situation is absurd. Isn't it?

With surprising difficulty, he raised himself up from the ground.

My back is getting worse, I feel so stiff. This isn't like me!

He realised that he was now standing in a soft carpet of grass which covered his slippers and reached up beyond the hem of his trouser bottoms. Each blade must now be at least twelve centimetres high. As he looked down, the grass was continuing to grow, even more rapidly. He was sure it had added another five centimetres in the last few minutes. He looked up at the sky. It had darkened even more.

Perhaps if I go inside these changes will stop.

He had no reason to think that. He just didn't understand what was going on, and so was trying to think of a way to reverse the process.

Maybe if I go indoors? But why should that make any difference? Mickey Abrahams was extremely bewildered.

He made a decision. He picked up the Shiva chair. It was heavier than he remembered. He had to push his way through the lawn. It was more difficult than he would have liked, and he felt abnormally tired. Suddenly it was night-time, and then quickly it became early morning light. The grass had suddenly sprung up with a burst of energy. It was now almost up to his knees. He had to struggle to wade through it and across to the paving that led to the French windows and into the lounge. The sky had quickly darkened again.

What's going on?

Mickey stood there looking up as the sky rapidly faded up to light, then faded down to dark. He went inside, carefully placed the Shiva chair on the floor and slumped down. His back was aching worse than ever. His bones felt weary. For the first time he noticed his hands. They looked creased, pitted and worn. His clothes suddenly felt loose on his body.

The French windows were still open, and he looked

outside. Everything was flashing, a stroboscopic event, as night became morning, became night, became morning, night, morning, night, morning.

He looked out and noticed the paint on the garage door, originally a bright blue.

The paint. It's peeled into flakes of faded colour.

It had taken him but a few minutes to go inside the house. In that time the grass had sprouted monstrously. It was now so high he was reminded of the song from a musical show.

What was the name of that damned show? How did the song go? "The something is as high as an elephant's something?"

His memory seemed to be failing him. What he did know was that if the grass continued growing at this most alarming rate, it wouldn't be long before it reached up to the tops of the doors.

But what was that? Sounds like a voice?

He thought he heard someone calling out to him from upstairs. He listened, but he couldn't be sure.

Mickey was stupefied. He had no explanation for what was happening. He didn't know what to do. Who could he phone? He wasn't even sure if it was allowed for a mourner to phone anyone during the Shiva week. Mickey wasn't a religious man. He kept the basics of his faith but didn't know all the ins and outs. Was that the voice calling out again? It sounded distressed. But again, he wasn't sure. With all this weird stuff going on, he had begun to feel that he couldn't trust his state of mind.

Anyway, there's no one else in the house except Eli. The others won't be arriving until the evening, for the Shivah service.

Mickey stood there shaking. He wondered where Eli was. The boy would probably be disturbed to see what was going on outside. Or rather, what had been going on. For as Mickey thought of his son, he noticed through the window, that the grass seemed to have stopped growing. But he also observed something that struck him as more sinister. The colour of the blades had changed from the vibrant green to a dull straw colour, as if the grass was drying up, as if it were dying.

This is really mad. What am I living through here?

He called his son. His voice came out weaker than normal. But then what was normal?

"Eli, where are you? Come to me please."

Silence.

"Eli, my boy. Come along. Would you like a cup of tea?"

And then Mickey Abrahams heard a voice. He didn't recognise it as his son's voice. It sounded far too deep. Who was in the house?

"Dad, I had to wear this stuff. I couldn't fit into my own clothes. What has happened to me?" Then Eli saw his father. "My god. Dad what has happened to you?"

Mickey nearly collapsed in dismay. Who was this man? Was that his son? At first, Eli was barely recognisable. The five-year-old had been transformed into a balding male of five foot ten, chubby in the middle, speaking in an adult voice. Like the grass, he had shot up. And he had aged, maturing in the space of a few hours. It was only because Eli openly acknowledged his father, that Mickey was able to discern a mirror image of himself at a similar age. And he noticed the small scar just below the right eye. On the way to the cinema, a few months before, Eli had decided to see what it would be like to be blind. He had closed his eyes. He had walked into a wall. The scar was a result of this misadventure. And as he recognised his son, Mickey realised that it must have been Eli in utter grief, calling out from upstairs.

"Father, what has happened here? The grass. Just look at it. What is going on with the two of us? Just look at yourself."

Eli reached up to the wall and removed the covering from a looking glass.

They saw themselves. Eli appeared to be in his forties, but the father was an old man, well into his eighties. His hair, once a jet black, was a yellowy white, wispy, lifeless. His skin was in folds, eyes, tired and listless. His body shrunken and stooped. His clothes hung from a frail figure. Mickey Abrahams observed himself and his boy in total disbelief.

And then it came to him, unannounced, like the bursting of the aneurism that had robbed him of his wife. Suddenly the confusion and anxiety seemed to clear from his mind, and the answer came to him. He knew now what had been happening to the lawn, to the rapid passing of days into nights, and to Eli and himself. Finally he could see it all, in sharp focus, like the blades of grass, when he had bent down to observe them closely. He realised what had occurred before, in the garden, as he'd woken up. The touching of his head.

It must have been. He'd tried to behave as a good Jew, had kept the Shiva for his dear Esther. And back there, in the garden, he felt the hand of God gently kissing his hair.

The Lord had visited the house of the Shiva and blessed Mickey and Eli. He'd made time fly. Like the green grass, they'd rapidly aged. And now, like the yellowing grass, he was withering away. Eli had some years yet to live, but Mickey knew that he was near death. God had seen to it that he would soon join his darling wife up there in heaven. Eli would follow later to join his beloved parents. Mickey was certain of that.

There was one problem for Mickey. As he looked again in the mirror, and saw his aged, wizened form, the old man couldn't help feeling apprehensive. Perhaps Eli should have left the cover on the mirror for the last night of Shiva. Perhaps they would be punished for removing it before the proper time?

For Mickey's thoughts had turned again to his departed wife. Esther was beautiful when she died. But now, he was ugly.

Would she still want to know me? Would she still fancy me?

He quickly replaced the cover over the mirror and turned to his son for comfort.

Arbadacarba

George Edward Humphries was no ordinary boy. In 1893, at the age of twelve he dazzled his schoolfriends with his expertise in performing tricks where his sleight of hand would fox them all.

"Which cup is the penny under?"

George Edward challenged his chum, Thomas Creighton. They were in the classroom, gathered round the teacher's desk.

"The middle one. I watched you carefully. It's under the middle one."

"Wrong again."

George Edward grinned as he lifted the cup to reveal the empty desktop. Just desktop, no penny.

"That's a penny you owe me!"

His classmates clapped loudly.

"So where is the penny?" Tony Davenport called out.

"Why, it's here," said George Edward, as he reached behind Tony's ear and pulled forth a shining coin.

More applause.

"Show us some more," his chums called out. Every one of his class pupils was George Edward's chum, he was immensely popular at school. But there wasn't time for more tricks, as they could hear Mr Cummings opening the classroom door. The boys rushed to their seats. Magic was over for the day.

Some years later, a master of ceremonies stepped forward onto the stage of the Empire Theatre in Hackney.

"Ladies and Gentlemen. And now for his first appearance at the Empire, here in the colourful East End of our wonderful capital city of London, in the glorious land of England. I bring you, at great expense to the theatre management, and for your delight, amusement and amazement, the youngest prestidigitator of renown in the entire universe, the master of the noble art of trickery, the most original practitioner of his profession, the greatest illusionist that has ever graced this magnificent, this most prestigious theatre of theatres, the one and only, the incomparable, the prince, no, the king of magicians."

The announcer paused, the audience gasped as they saw a figure appear at the back of the stage, in a halo of green light.

"Ladies and gentlemen, I give to you… the Great Enrico Maldini!"

George Edward Humphries stepped forward to loud applause and cheering. For it was he, now a well-built, precocious twenty-one-year-old, who masqueraded as the Italian conjurer.

The orchestra in the theatre pit struck up an operatic melody featuring violins and a chorus of female singers. Maldini was wearing a tomato-red robe made of the finest silks, worn over a pair of bright white pants, which flared from the knee, and a matching loose fitting, white tunic shirt. From under the pants could be seen the edges of a pair of green silk boots. On his head was a cap of green. He wore the colours of the Italian flag. The music grew more intense rising to a crescendo as the Great Maldini came to the front of the stage and took a long, low bow. The audience continued to applaud. He hadn't shown them a thing yet. Not one trick. It was all reputation. Despite being so young, Enrico Maldini had in the space of a few years, built himself a monstrous reputation for his magical performances amongst the patrons of variety theatres in London and Europe.

Decades later, the comic magician, Tommy Cooper would appear onstage and on television, and the audiences would

93

collapse in laughter just at the sight of him, and before he had performed a trick. But that was different. Maldini had a mysterious appearance, not at all funny. Tommy Cooper always looked hugely funny. His red fez, his huge, pasty potato face, his hulking frame. Tommy's very awkwardness would raise a laugh. And when he uttered his catchphrase "Just like that" in a voice which sounded as if he had just chain smoked a dozen fags, the crowd would crease up in mirth. And he hadn't really done anything yet!

But Tommy Cooper's style of comedy magic was a sophisticated, if quirky, interpretation; a step along the evolutionary spectrum of the magician's art which practitioners like Maldini had helped to popularise all those years before. It is Enrico Maldini's story, we shall follow in this tale.

George Edward Humphries had decided on his vocation at an early age, while still at Saint Michael's Grammar school, in Hornsey, North London. Several years later he became Enrico Maldini because he realised that the magic, the tricks, would not be enough to project him towards the fame he craved.

During his schooldays, he often accompanied his parents on their travels to America and Europe. He would go to the theatres with them, to see, amongst other entertainments, the famous magicians of the day. In 1888, at the impressionable age of just seven, he saw the Great Alexander Herrmann perform his new illusions, The Black Art and Le Cocon at the 5th Avenue Theatre and at Niblo's Garden in New York.

The boy was highly impressionable, and he was totally overwhelmed by the illusions he witnessed. He vowed to become a magician himself, and to devote his time to mastering the necessary arts and skills to become such an entertainer. But the boy would not be happy with becoming an ordinary performer. His ambition was to be the best. After seeing several other shows, George Edward realised that he must develop an individual approach to presenting his developing art. He needed an image that would intrigue and entrance. Italy and Italians fascinated him, for his father engaged in trade in Italy and had built a summer home in Tuscany. The young George Edward was sometimes taken by his father to visit the factories around San Giminianno, specialising in Italian ceramics, and he spent most of his summer holidays at the house near Poggibonsi. He became fluent in Italian. And so the idea for Enrico Maldini, the Italian magician, was born, and George Edward, when he performed, adopted the clothes and mannerisms of his alter ego.

When he spoke onstage it was with a good enough Italian accent for the audience to believe that he was indeed from that country. And he always had the orchestra play arias from the more popular Italian operas. By the time of his debut appearance at the Hackney Empire, he had perfected a number of magical illusions. As in any form of popular entertainment, it behoves the artist to satisfy the expectations of his audience, both for the familiar, and for the surprise. For most of the top magicians the tricks were about putting new wine into old bottles.

Over two thousand people attended the Hackney Empire that night, expecting to see certain tricks for which the illusionist was famous but with some new inflections. Occasionally something really different would happen, and a new departure in the language of magic; a technical breakthrough, an original idea, or both would be announced. There were to be no such radical tricks on that evening, though the show did intrigue and delight its audience.

Maldini's first offerings were graceful little conjuring tricks, where deft movements of his elegant hands created flowers from strips of silky fabrics, which, with a flick became live white rabbits. A charming petite young female assistant, in robes of bright red hue, stepped forward, and with a delicate bow, handed the master a large dish. He showed the dish to the audience. The front rows saw it to be empty. The magician tilted the dish and waved it around to allow the middle and back rows, and those in the dress circle, to see the empty dish. The drummer played a drum roll. The Great Maldini whirled around and around, faster and faster, in a mad circular motion. The drummer increased the intensity of his rhythm. It was extraordinary that Maldini kept his balance, as he whirled like a dervish around the stage, the dish held at arm's length. Suddenly he stopped, the drum roll continued, the assistant came forward, holding a clear glass jar for all to see. Maldini stepped towards her, and to the delight of all present in the theatre, poured from his dish, blood red wine, filling the jar to the brim.

A second assistant, a young Sicilian boy, in bright green and white robes, presented some goblets to the maestro, who filled them with wine, and handed them back to the two assistants. With admirable composure, the two young helpers left the stage to present the goblets of a fine Chianti to members of the audience fortunate enough to have front row seats. The orchestra struck up the well-known *Torna a Sorrento*, and the applause from the crowd could be heard along Mare Street, which fronted the Hackney Empire.

As the years went by George Edward Humphries developed his art. It was typical of the magic business for the conjurers to steal new illusions from those who introduced them. So, taking out a patent on one's idea was critical. Not that it always stopped the practice of stealing.

96

George Edward had seen the Black Art, which had been performed since the 1870's if not before. This was a most wonderfully contrived illusion where things would suddenly appear on the stage, and sometimes disappear from the audience's view.

What happened in this technique depended on a clever optical effect, where objects looked as if they appeared or disappeared. The objects covered in black materials, a table, a chair, a vase and even people, dressed all in black, including faces and hands covered in black make-up, were positioned in front of a dense black background, so that there was no shadow. Lights were strategically arranged on the stage. Other lights, just beneath the stage, shone into the audience but didn't throw light on the stage itself. The effect was to create the illusion, black objects and performers being invisible against black background.

Maldini had seen a number of conjurors present episodes of the Black Art. He wanted this technique for himself and so he copied it and used it in the theatres. His special assistant, all in black, and with the background and lights cleverly set, rendered so she was invisible to the audience, would bring a vase covered in black fabric onto the stage. The covered-up vase melted into the black background. It could not be seen by the crowd.

Maldini, his voice booming; the accent Italian, dramatically announced the words, "Abracadabra, Arbadacarba." The assistant swiftly removed the black sheet and behold, a vibrantly-coloured yellow vase appeared, where none had been before.

As word spread, it seemed that his reputation grew exponentially. By the end of the Great War, George Edward Humphries's act as the Italian magician, was famous all over Europe and in America. He had played Paris, Rome, Berlin, New York and Boston to name just a few major centres. Back home he triumphed, amongst other cities and towns, in London, Sheffield, Blackpool, Nottingham, Birmingham, Manchester Leeds and Liverpool.

He performed a variety of tableaux based on the Black Art, making objects, people and animals appear as if from nowhere. His most famous trick was to make a lion appear on the stage. The lion, of course, had been adequately sedated and its trainer, suitably decked out in black, complicit in the performance.

Maldini loved to make his announcements in his fake Italian accent, placing the stress on certain syllables, to impress the audience that he was indeed from that Mediterranean country.

"Ladeeze ana gentlemena. Zee Great Maldini, merviglioso magiccione, gonna now showa to you, zee most tremendoso illuzzione. Izza gonna bee fantastico."

Then he would step forward and by deft legerdemain, would produce bottles of vino rosso from thin air, and steaming hot dishes of pasta from behind his ears, ready for his assistant to hand out to the front rows. It became part of the Maldini publicity to advertise that if you were hungry, you should make sure you got to sit in the front row, where you should, with luck, be well fed, or at least given a glass of quality Chianti. Possibly both.

After a few years, however, he abandoned the fake accent. He completely stopped addressing his audience. The rumour was spread that he had lost his voice in an accident. The reality was that Maldini had begun to realise that as popular as he was, he might benefit from increasing the element of mystique in his act. This objective was helped when he married a voluptuous, beautiful, yet slightly sinister-looking female assistant, known, appropriately as Bella Donna, who would occasionally perform some weird magic and could make any necessary announcements.

George Edward had attended a number of performances by the great oriental illusionist Chung Ling Soo, who never uttered a word on stage. The magician wasn't really oriental, he was American. However, George Edward was impressed by the all-pervading air of mystery when Chung Ling enacted his magic routines. So, from that time on, to increase even further the mystique of his shows, Maldini made no announcements, and the public swallowed the story of his vocal impediment.

He was not satisfied with becoming a most important magician on the European stage. George Edward was a dreamer. His most fervent dream was to be able to predict the future. He cherished the idea of making predictions in his show, which would be reported in the press as having happened by the time of a subsequent show on a set date in a month's time. In this respect he seemed unable to distinguish between magic, as the creation of clever illusions, each of which seemed so authentic that his audiences took them for reality, and his fantasy of discovering the key to telling the future. It might be said that he was losing his grip on reality, and indeed this was the opinion of many in the magic fraternity to whom he had unwisely boasted that he would soon be able to make accurate predictions in this manner.

But he worked hard on the idea. He studied Nostradamus, who'd been credited with predicting the Great Fire of London and the rise of Napoleon. His studies were to no avail. He never learned how to make the predictions from his readings of the seer. He studied astrology. Again, no use. He just didn't acquire the confidence to be sure of making accurate predictions. He tried interpreting dreams, he tried numerology and water divining. None of them gave him what he sought. He was never able to achieve his cherished goal. So, he dropped the idea and settled for second best, a trick of mind reading by clever use of an assistant.

The assistant would approach a member of the audience and ask questions, requiring a single word answer which could not be heard by the magician on the stage. By careful use of language, the assistant called out the answer, in a coded manner, enabling the magician to "read" the mind of the subject. Maldini would then write the answers in bold illuminated letters on a special board for all to see. It was clever but it wasn't telling the future, and he knew it was a poor substitute and something seemed to snap in him. He had lost face because of his failure to achieve the skill which he had boasted to fellow magicians he would soon master.

Although Maldini was unable to tell the future, the future would happen, and it would bring on the one hand, scientific discoveries and technological innovations, and on the other, elegant theories of time, space and the cosmos which the Great Maldini, were he to have been around from the nineteen thirties until the year this tale is being written, might have thought were magic of the most outrageous kind. But the conjurer was locked into his time frame, from the last decade of the nineteenth century until his curious and unaccounted for disappearance in 1921.

He tried to put aside his obsession with the future. After a few weeks of depression, when he turned down some important bookings, the illusionist picked himself up. He was still the Great Maldini. He would triumph over adversity, and he had the delicious Bella Donna by his side. He loved her so much.

But the wave on which the Great Maldini had ridden high began to ebb. At first it was a series of mistakes of his timing onstage, or poor preparation by his assistants where cracks appeared in the Black Art illusions. Hurriedly-applied make-up, or black clothing that had got caught in some props and revealed the assistant's pale hand,or ankle, showed the front rows that there seemed to be an extra person on the platform. Members of the audience, especially in those front rows that might still be glad of the free goblet of wine and the pasta bowl, could see something of how the trick was performed. The sleight of hand when glasses were slipped to Maldini's black gloved hand didn't quite work when the fingers of the assistant could be seen. Those in the audience who received the free drink from Bella Donna would be heard to mutter and mumble, "Look you can see the fingers. I know how he does it!"

Then there was a series of incidents on stage which were far more worrying. Maldini convinced Bella Donna and his other assistants that he had finally perfected the art of fire-eating. He had been trying to get this right for several years. They weren't convinced, and urged him to practise further. He wilfully ignored their caution. The second time he performed his fire-eating routine, it went horribly wrong, and he singed his black locks and nearly set fire to his robes. Water had to be thrown over him and the stage curtains rapidly drawn.

Another time, when they appeared at the Alhambra Theatre in London's Leicester Square, Bella Donna fell through a trapdoor set into the stage floor. The door had sprung open before time, taking her by surprise as she lay cramped inside the box, previously shown to be empty, ready to jump out to the applause of the audience. This part of the illusion wasn't remarkable. What made the piece more interesting was that the audience had just witnessed Bella Donna being sawn in half by Maldini himself. But the trick backfired. The unfortunate Bella Donna cracked a bone in her left foot as she landed awkwardly under the stage floor.

It was when Maldini failed to catch the silver bullet in his teeth that he decided to give up the stage and take an early retirement. Normally Bella Donna would fire the gun at him, though there would be no bullet inside, as it had been expertly palmed. The bullet had been selected by a member of the audience from a box of six silver bullets handed him by the second assistant. It had then been carefully marked by the volunteer. However, Maldini was secretly given an identical silver bullet, surreptitiously marked by the second assistant, in exactly the same manner as the one Bella Donna had palmed. At a strategic moment, when the audience's attention was concentrated on the pistol, the illusionist had inserted his bullet into his mouth, ready to show between his teeth.

The gun was fired, and a real bullet whizzed across the stage just grazing Maldini's left temple. He had narrowly escaped death. Had Bella Donna really palmed the bullet? Had she inserted it into the gun, determined to assassinate her husband? Or had someone else made the switch, and if so, how? The truth is that no one ever discovered the truth, despite police investigations, where all involved were rigorously questioned. Bella Donna denied inserting the bullet into the gun, claiming that she had palmed it and indeed removing a marked silver bullet from a pocket in her robe and showing it to the Inspector.

Had there been a third marked bullet, and had the gun containing it been switched for the original weapon? We will never know because the police, having drawn a blank, (an appropriate metaphor it seems), halted the interrogation. Maldini was physically unharmed, the police had no clues. They didn't know if a crime had been committed, or it was simply an accident. Maldini himself urged that the show must go on. As it did on the following night.

But the Great Maldini had lost the plot. This final misadventure hadn't harmed him physically, but psychologically it wrought great damage. And taken together with the other recent mishaps, it seemed like a warning. He'd had a good run, he was still young, wealthy and in love with Bella Donna, never for one moment believing her to have tried to murder him. He would retire from the stage. They would travel the world together. Despite the recent accidents, he was still the Great Maldini – was he not? He would be feted in all the major cities across the globe. Life would be sweet. But he would perform one last show.

On September the 14th, 1921 George Edward Humphries appeared at the Empire Wood Green, the magnificent theatre in north London where he had first appeared at the aged of eighteen. It was billed as the Great Maldini's last performance. Bella Donna was with him, as were three other assistants. During his act, sometimes between tricks, at other times during an illusion, the orchestra played selected excerpts from famous arias, and special musical effects to heighten the tension as appropriate. There was to be a surprise champagne party after the show. Maldini and his troupe would join in with the guests, many of them specially invited from the world of theatre magic.

Maldini excelled himself that evening. His sleight of hand was unbelievable. He turned flowers into dogs, which appeared suddenly from who knew where. He then picked up one of the dogs while Bella Donna carried the others off stage. By the time she reappeared, he'd turned the remaining dog into a bunch of flowers again. He made a simple copper penny become a shower of gold coins.

Then he walked among the front row of the audience pulling cards from pockets, gold watches from behind ears, little kittens from ladies' corsages.

Back on the stage he went through a fire-eating routine,

without mishap, and performed various Black Art scenarios with Bella Donna, making her disappear and reappear in a number of set pieces. Then he sawed her into quarters, after which, when she had reappeared in one piece, he levitated her several feet above the stage.

There was a loud drum roll. At last it was time for his finale. Silence from the musicians in the pit, as for the first time the Great Maldini came near the front of the stage and spoke directly to the audience. It was the voice, the refined English middle-class accent of George Edward Humphries, that rang out across the theatre. Most in the audience were shocked when they heard him announcing.

"Ladies and gentlemen, my esteemed colleagues, friends and guests. All of you here tonight. Thank you for joining Bella Donna, myself and my valued assistants, for our final show. My art has been to try to achieve perfect illusions for your delight, and my life too has contained elements of illusion, for as you see I am not the Italian personage most of you suppose. I am an Englishman, George Edward Humphries, proud to be so, and proud to have been for the best part of twenty-five years a member of this most illustrious profession of magic."

He paused for dramatic effect. And then, increasing the intensity of his declaration, uttered his final words.

"And now I leave you for a different life."

The drummer played out a rhythm, which increased in volume as the action unfolded. The Great Maldini stepped back and climbed up a set of steps towards the front of a large cabinet that suddenly appeared, suspended from on high, and floating over the stage. A set of doors swung open. The audience could see inside, there was nothing. The cabinet appeared empty. They also saw that, as it was raised above the stage, there could be no means of vacating the cabinet undetected by means of a trap door. Maldini stepped inside and turning to face the audience, held out his arms, his delicate palms pointed upwards towards the heavens, and in a loud voice that boomed out across the auditorium, uttered the words, "Abracadabra Arbadacarba!"

The cabinet doors were immediately shut. The drummer commenced another drum roll.

The Great Maldini was supposed to disappear from inside the cabinet. He was supposed to vanish, leaving Bella Donna and the three assistants pretending to be in a state of confusion and consternation. This is indeed what Maldini did. He disappeared. The cabinet was lowered onto the stage, the doors swung open to reveal that the conjurer had gone. Bella and the others on stage, as they were supposed to do, acted most surprised and concerned. It was all part of the act. After a few minutes when everyone seemed not to know what to expect, when the audience were shuffling in their seats, talking amongst themselves. "Should we stay? Should we go? What's happening?" Maldini was supposed to reappear, in front of the first row of seats, to join his guests at the champagne celebration. Indeed, a group of waiters and waitresses suitably dressed in the red, white and green of Italy appeared at the rear of the Empire, wheeling in trolleys with all kinds of tasty international dishes and bottles of Champagne, wines and spirits.

It was Bella Donna who stepped forward. as planned, still on the stage, but no longer acting anxious at the disappearance of her husband.

"Dear guests, please make your way to the back of the theatre for our celebration. My darling husband will soon join us."

And everyone filed back up the aisles to partake of the

feast. Minutes passed, The Great Maldini was nowhere to be seen in the theatre. Certainly not celebrating his retirement with his invited guests. A large golden goblet of champagne, had just been poured for him in the certainty that he would process up the aisle from the front of the theatre, that the goblet would be handed to him by an exquisitely dressed assistant, and that he would join his guests in a final toast to his career. This did not happen.

An act of God? A ripple on the fabric of space-time? An unknown gateway from inside the magic cabinet of specially contrived mirrors, opening up into a parallel universe? One thing certain is that what took place was truly a piece of magic beyond all magic. The Great Maldini never walked from the stage up the aisle, and never joined the party at the back of the auditorium of the Empire Theatre. Two hours after his disappearance, all the guests had left in a quandary, completely bemused as to their hero's whereabouts. Bella Donna had been stricken with anxiety and had already summoned a policeman. It was the same policeman who had questioned her at the Alhambra. By a curious coincidence, he had been reassigned to a post in the Wood Green police force.

Somewhere, onstage, in another universe, the Great Maldini found himself facing the audience from the entrance, just inside a magic cabinet suspended above the stage, ready to disappear from sight. He looked at the front rows. As before, he pointed his outstretched palms upwards towards the heavens, his voice booming out across the auditorium, and uttered the magic mirror image words, "Abracadabra Arbadacarba."

The cabinet doors were closed, the drum roll begun. The cabinet was lowered, the doors were reopened, and once more the magician had disappeared from inside, and the audience was left gasping in amazement, but ready to celebrate the illusionist's quick return.

He never returned. Time passed, the audience were leaving the theatre, an anxious Bella Donna had called the policeman.

Nor did Maldini return to any of the audiences after he uttered the forward backward magic incantation and played out the episode of his final disappearance, as in a loop of a video recording. There is no published record of how and why this happened, but the Great Maldini and his audience found themselves caught up inside a web of parallel universes, like the multiple reflections from a pair of boundless cosmic mirrors which face each other across space. For soon after he had disappeared from inside the cabinet, he reappeared again, again and again, ad infinitum, and Bella Donna, the illusionist's three assistants, the policeman and the entire audience played out their parts in the sequence. Those present at that time and in that theatre space were all trapped, and only death would set them free. But within this complex of magic cabinets inside parallel universes, was death itself merely an illusion?

The Singer

It was April 1970 and Danny Silver had been in London just a week when he ran into Annie in Golders Green Road. He had left the north to escape his past, though he still owed money to some shady characters with whom he had once hung out. He hadn't seen her for a couple of years, but he recognised her immediately.

It's Annie from Leeds. I wonder what she is doing here in Golders Green.

"Hey, Annie, babe," he called out as he crossed the main street. He approached her and gave her a big hug.

"What's with you? Fancy seeing you here. How are you? What are you up to?"

"Hey, hey, calm down," Annie replied. "So many questions. Good to see you too, Danny. You have lost a bit of weight I think."

Danny had been going to the gym and had shed a few kilos. He was fair haired and quite tall, a fairly presentable twenty-nine-year-old with piercing blue eyes. The left one had a strange greenish cast, just a speck.

"Still teaching, still singing?" Annie asked.

"Yes to the first. No to the second. But tell me what brings you to London? Still looking for a nice Jewish husband?"

Annie would make someone a good Jewish wife. In the looking-after-her-man department she wasn't quite up to the dedication of John Beringer's mum, but not far off. Very near in fact! Danny shared a flat in Golder's Green with Johnny, who couldn't lift a finger to look after himself. Whenever his mum visited, she did everything for him, so Danny wasn't surprised at Johnny's indolence.

Annie Simmons was a plump girl. It would be kind to call her voluptuous. Danny considered her to be plump, that was the long and short of it. So he was a little taken aback when she told him what she was doing for work.

"I am working at the Palace club in the West End, one of Jim Morgan's places. I'm a hostess, topless!"

"Oooooh, you naughty girl," Danny replied, stifling a fit of laughter. *Mustn't be disrespectful to Annie. And she is well stacked on top. I should know!*

Danny had had a brief fling with Annie in Leeds a few years back, and he remembered her assets.

"Well, I guess it pays good money," he continued, as Annie, stood there, defiant looking.

"Yes it does. We get paid well to walk around topless, and I get terrific tips from a diamond merchant, and all I have to do is sit with him and serve him the Champagne. That's on top of the other tips and my basic wage. He's an old guy, harmless. Hasn't come on to me. Not once. Fact is I feel a bit sorry for him. He's just lonely, I guess. So no harm in what I do."

"Do you ever have to fight them off though?" Danny enquired. "The guys, I mean. There must be the occasional difficult situation."

"It's fine. Mr Morgan runs the place with clockwork efficiency. Any problems, the bouncers move in and eject the offending punter. We don't tolerate any form of abuse of the girls. Jim Morgan respects us all, treats us well, though he has his favourites."

Danny was to find out more about Jim Morgan's favourites a few weeks later.

"As it happens, we are looking for a vocalist to front the house trio, why don't you call in and fix up an audition?"

So that's what he did. Danny phoned the number Annie gave him and spoke to Vince, the manager, who arranged for him to sing a few tunes with the band. He suggested

Danny go down there that evening as they needed someone pretty quickly. However, when he phoned, Danny used a false name. He called himself Adam Steele. He didn't want anyone to know at work that he was moonlighting, nor did he want the club people to know he was a college teacher. Danny could be secretive.

Danny kept a black velvet suit in the wardrobe back at the flat. That evening he dressed, tried to look as smart as possible, had a quick chicken and chips at one of the restaurants on Golders Green Road, and drove down to the West End.

The Palace club, in Glasshouse Street, near Piccadilly was one of two clubs owned by Jim Morgan, and benefited from a late-night drinking licence. His other club, the Horseshoe, didn't, and so closed around midnight. The Palace went on until four in the morning. Jim Morgan arranged for cars to transport the crowd from the Horseshoe over to the Palace, those who wanted to continue drinking and dancing. He also had an arrangement with many of the West End cabbies to recommend his clubs to anyone looking for a good night who hailed a cab and asked where the best place was to unwind in the company of attractive females. Business in both venues was brisk.

Danny, now calling himself Adam, parked, and was soon being escorted inside the club by Freddie Gummins, ex wrestling champion who worked as a bouncer for Morgan. Freddie stood six foot, a weightlifter's body, jaw like a rock, and his voice rasped through years of smoking and alcohol. But he was friendly enough, and quickly escorted Adam to meet the manager, a tall, slim dark-haired man in his mid to late thirties. It was still early in the evening, around nine thirty, and so there were few customers. Adam

110

took in the scene, the garish, amber-coloured walls and low lighting; except for the area round the bar, which gleamed more brightly with a golden glow. The effect of the décor and lighting made him feel he was inside a huge golden ingot. The mood was one of flash luxury.

Vince took him over to a small, raised platform, the stage, set up with piano, double bass and a drum kit, and lit with a largish circular halo effect, which had been set up to change colour every few minutes. He was introduced to Tony Moxam, the band leader, who played piano, Pete Harrington on the string bass, and a wiry, intense-looking character, Dave Black, the drummer.

Adam was primarily a jazz singer, and a crooner of the many classic songs from the great composers of the thirties through to the fifties. He handed his sheet music to Tony, and the guys quickly launched into the first song, Cole Porter's *Night and Day*. Adam came in with the vocal after the intro. He quickly felt relaxed with the group. The tempo was right and the band swung along sweetly. Adam even received some applause at the end of the number. Then Tony upped the tempo and they went into Jerome Kern's *The Way You Look Tonight*, followed by *Nice Work If You Can Get It*, a Gershwin number. The music was partly to help create atmosphere, but also for dancing, especially the smoochy, slower tempo numbers, like *My Funny Valentine*, by Rodgers and Hart. Adam ended his audition with this song, though, at that time, nobody came on the floor to dance.

The guys took a short break, and Adam saw that Tony Moxam had gone over to talk to Vince. He went to the bar, ordered a scotch on the rocks, and waited nervously for the verdict about his performance.

The news was good. "Can you stay on and start tonight?" Tony said. "Have you enough material with you?"

111

"Sure. I brought in a stack of music. What's my pay?"

"Vince will sort that out with you. Here he comes now."

"As far as me and the band go, you're in, Adam," Vince said. "I only hope that Mr Morgan, approves. We will find out soon. No promises, but if he likes you, then we need you seven nights a week. He mentioned the money they would pay."

"Fine," Adam replied. That money, plus his teacher's salary would mean a decent lifestyle, so he knew he had to impress Jim Morgan when he came in.

"What's his favourite songs. Do you know?" Adam asked Vince.

"Mr Morgan likes Bobby Darin numbers."

"I can do *Dream Lover* and *Mack the Knife*, I have the sheet music with me. Is that okay?"

"Sure."

Vince turned and went over to talk with Tony, and they were soon joined by a short, dapper man, with slicked down, thinning dark hair, sallow complexion and thin lips. He wore a dark grey suit, black silk shirt and a silver tie. Adam was called over. Adam's first impression of Jim Morgan was of controlled violence, and he felt uneasy. But he didn't have to sing for Mr Morgan. There was no need for Bobby Darin songs that evening.

Morgan had been followed across the floor by a couple of glamorous females, one of whom was really beautiful, while the other, reasonable looking, was more noticeable for her cleavage. Vince introduced the singer.

"Adam Steele, meet Jim Morgan, the boss."

Not once did Morgan look directly at him. His shifty eyes glanced across Adam's face, and he talked towards some indeterminate point at the other side of the room. He said little, and soon turned his attention to Amanda, the beautiful one.

"Let's hope this singer is better than the last." Then he steered the two girls over to the bar. But the threesome soon left the premises.

Adam found out later that Morgan had been sitting quietly at the back of the club, heard the audition, and instructed Vince to hire him. Adam didn't see the boss again for a couple of weeks. He felt no displeasure at Morgan's absence, and had taken an instant dislike to the man. For all his dapper style, to the singer, the boss man looked sleazy.

That first night, the Palace filled up, mostly with business types and the occasional dolled-up, tarty-looking female. Adam's performance attracted measured applause, but he felt that he had impressed the guys in the band, and that was good enough. Despite its air of luxury, the Palace wasn't high class. The hostesses went round the tables, sitting with the punters, encouraging them to buy over-priced bottles of Champagne, occasionally taking to the dance floor where the man got close, leaning into the girl, whispering in her ear. Some of the hostesses were topless.

Adam felt uncomfortable. He thought the ladies friendly and helpful, but disliked this display of what seemed to be available flesh for sale. But he remembered what Annie had told him, and as he worked nights at the club, he never saw any of the girls looking as if they wanted out of the place. Except one very special girl. Sylvia Campbell. But that came later.

Annie worked a couple of nights a week and introduced him to all the hostesses. He had briefed her about his new name, and she played along. As he got to know them better it was made clear that the hostesses felt they were exploiting the men, rather than the other way round. A few of girls had young children and were working to earn enough extra to help raise them. The tips were good. In some cases, as Annie had explained, very good. What the girls did after they left the club was their business. But Adam's impression was that it was rare for any of them to go off with the punters. He got to like most of them, and fancied one or two.

He worked at the Palace seven nights a week, and during the day, at the college, where he was employed teaching chemistry. He told no one about his double life. Danny Silver by day, Adam Steele, by night. He had opened a bank account under his stage name and his earnings, paid in cash, went straight into it. Things were looking up. Adam had put the past behind. The disturbances of his younger days were fading. He had managed to pay off some of his debts.

He decided to move out of the Golders Green pad, John Beringer was impossible. He had far too many girls back in his room, and the place was fast becoming a tip. Items of female clothing littered the floor in the lounge and hung from the towel rail in the bathroom. God knows what Johnny's bedroom was like! One thing about Adam, he was scrupulously tidy. But he felt like he was being crowded out and was pleased he had decided to move out to his own place. He and Johnny would occasionally meet up at the Bull and Bush.

Adam rented a small studio flat in Belsize Square, with a parking space. He could afford it now that he had the moonlighting gig. Besides he wanted some privacy. It would be better for his love life if he lived on his own. When he had chatted to them, a couple of the girls at the Palace had indicated interest in him, said they liked his singing and thought he seemed a genuine nice guy. He wasn't sure whether to go for Renate, a German hostess, with soft skin and deep dark eyes, or a small Scottish lass,

Sylvia Campbell, a delightful creature with golden hair and wonderful voice, clear and gentle sounding with lovely Scottish inflections. Sylvia wasn't a hostess, she mostly worked the bar.

Adam acted boldly and dated both girls. He was upfront about the situation and told them he wanted to take out both of them, see which one worked the best for him, and if he was a man either of them might want. The two girls appreciated his honesty. Both said they understood where he was coming from and they accepted what they felt would be a temporary situation, though it might become longer lasting for one of them. He realised he was being cheeky, but at least he felt he was being open with Renate and Sylvia, and he never tried it on with them at the same time. They just arranged a few dates in a sequence, which enabled Adam to see each in turn over a two-week period.

Renate, though she was very sexy, turned out to be a slob. She and John Beringer would have made the perfect pair, he thought, but never introduced them. Typically, John had enough on his plate.

So Adam soon struck up a relationship with Sylvia. She had a small son, William. Adam really took to the boy. Sylvia had explained that William's father had recently run out on them. The three seemed to get on famously. She was warm and giving, sensitive, and though she was a slip of a girl, he found her enticing. William was just fun. There was a kind of mystery to Sylvia, which was a turn on. But there was something else about her, which he couldn't explain, but which made him feel protective.

A couple of months after he started at the Palace, he was in the club and had just come off the stage after the second set of

115

songs. It must have been around midnight. Vince called him over to the bar, ordered him a double scotch on the rocks. Morgan had recently opened a new club somewhere on the coast, near Southend. Vince wanted Adam to work there, at least for the next few weeks, to help establish the music scene. They had a band lined up, a quartet: piano, saxophone, bass and drums. He indicated it might become a more regular gig, and that Adam might have to relocate to the area. They would see that he had first-rate accommodation.

Adam was completely unprepared for this, and for the moment was lost for what to say. He must have muttered something about thinking it over, needing time to think. Something like that.

"Don't take too long," Vince replied. "Mr Morgan will be in soon. He needs an answer, tonight!"

Adam urgently needed another drink. Sylvia, still working the bar, poured a second scotch. He grabbed it and sank back onto one of the plush velvet seats. He needed to think. He tried to concentrate. The chatter from the punters, the sound of glasses tinkling, made it hard for him to focus. What could he do? He had the teaching job. No way could he walk out on that. So far he had been lucky and been able to handle both gigs, even though he often got back home in the small hours, grabbed five hours sleep before going into a full day's work at the college. Then it would start over again. Get back to the flat, shower and shave, change into the velvet suit or a newer, snazzy cream outfit. Then a bite to eat. If Sylvia was around she might prepare a snack, otherwise it would be a local café.

Drive down to the club, and onstage for the evening. Four music sets. It was tiring work, but he was young and had boundless energy. True, his love life with Sylvia was suffering. Sometimes they had little time together before one or both had to get off to work. And Sylvia had young

William to look after. Despite his dislike of Jim Morgan, who increasingly struck him as creepy, the singer really didn't want to lose this gig. It paid well, more than he would normally expect from club gigs, and he needed the money to pay off his debts. But he couldn't give up his regular career in teaching. Being a full-time club singer was just too precarious.

These concerns raced through Adam's mind as he tried to think of a way round the problem Vince had thrown at him. Then it dawned on him. Why had it taken so long to realise? End of term. Summer vacation from college. He had a couple of months when he didn't have to go in to teach. He could give the Southend club eight weeks or so. Vince indicated that the money would be really good. If Adam saved enough, maybe he and Sylvia could work out a way of leaving Jim Morgan and his club scene. Maybe they could rely on Adam's day job and the odd bar work they might both get. They would have to pay a child minder to look after William. They would be able to spend more time together. He really wanted this and believed that Sylvia did too. And he was getting close to William, really loved the kid.

When Morgan came into the club and called Adam over for his decision on the new job, the matter proved more contentious. Vince had told Adam what his wages would be at Southend. He had promised it was going to be big money!

"So you are going to be with us at my new club? What do you say?" Morgan greeted him, eyes darting everywhere but in Adam's direction.

"Yes, why not? Vince told me the wages."

"Well, I just talked to Vince, he got the money wrong." Morgan's tone hardened. "It will be half what he said for the first week, until I am sure you go down well there. Then I will see about a raise."

Adam was momentarily shaken, but felt he had to stand firm. "Mr Morgan, I can't do it for that. I was told more. That's what I agreed with Vince."

Morgan went wild. The only time he looked Adam in the face. When he conversed with women he would look directly at them. This was the one time Adam saw him look straight at a man. He was in a flaming temper, and for some reason could direct his eyes into him. They pierced through him, a castrating stare.

"Vince!" He spat out the name. "Do you think Vince runs things? I run things. Me, the boss. The guy who pays the bills. And you do what you are told or you are out! Get me?"

Adam's reaction to this outburst was rapid. He kept his cool. He would stick it out in the Southend club for eight weeks. The money, even though less than he had been told, was still more than they were paying him at the Palace. It would make it worthwhile, especially if he got the raise. He would be able to pay the rest of his debts to the guys in the north. Then he and Sylvia would quit.

But Morgan's aggression caused something to twist inside him. That's when the serious trouble started which was to result in Adam reviving something dark from Danny Silver's past. But because Adam had the gall to argue over wages, Morgan decided to resurrect something from his own past to humiliate him.

What Adam Steele didn't know at the time was that Jim Morgan had a thing for Sylvia. Jim Morgan had a habit for women, period. But his obsession was to lure a few, scrupulously-selected girls, into nights of debauched sex. Adam didn't know how he did it. Maybe it was his money, perhaps the girls were afraid he would get rid of them from

118

the club. Maybe Morgan just knew how to tune into those who were similarly depraved.

Morgan was a sex control obsessive. He arranged sessions back at his mansion in Finchley, which he, or his guests photographed. Morgan and Vince, Helen, (Vince's wife), Olivia, she of the cleavage, and Fiona, a tall slim, sometimes topless hostess, could occasionally be seen, huddled in a corner of the club, in semi-shadow, flicking through lewd images taken a few nights before.

Adam never saw the pictures, but it was clear to him from their body language, leaning into and across each other, touching each other, the raucous laughter, and sexy phrases, that the group were showing off photos of their wanton antics at their previous drunken session together at Morgan's place.

Soon after the incident over the Southend gig, Morgan called him over. The boss was sitting with Sylvia. She looked ashen, distant, shrunken up into herself. Morgan was leafing through some photos.

"You wanna see what we have?" Come and look at your friend Sylvia here. Bet you haven't seen her like this." As he approached, Adam caught a whiff of alcohol. Typically, Morgan's watery grey eyes were looking past the singer.

"No thanks," muttered Adam. Morgan had moved towards Sylvia in the corner, put his hand on her thigh, and was stroking it almost up to her panty line. Adam felt sick. He turned and made off to the bar. He was shaking. He leaned heavily against the counter, propping himself up. He downed a double brandy. Then called for another.

That night, Sylvia failed to return to the flat. Adam couldn't sleep. He raged at the thought of Morgan and the others perverting his golden-haired child, as he had begun to think of her. Adam was seriously wound up inside. The morning came. He heard the key turn in the front door.

Sylvia crept into the room. He was awake. He needed to find out the nature and extent of her involvement with Morgan. Had she been fooling him all along? Was she just a slut?

She approached the bed. She broke down sobbing violently.

"He made me do things, Morgan did. He threatened to take the boy away. Adam I never said before, but Jim Morgan is my boy's father!"

Adam recoiled. He could not have conceived of this scenario. The thought made his stomach churn.

"He can do these things. You don't know him. How far he will go. Years ago, he raped me, and William is the result of that. And now he has designs on William too. He is just a beast. I don't know what to do. He hasn't touched him yet, but threatens me that if I don't satisfy his needs he will molest the boy."

Now Adam knew why Sylvia looked so uncomfortable, flinching at Morgan's touch that night at the Palace; the night the boss called him over to show his appalling photographs.

Something broke inside. Images from his past in the North of England flooded into his mind, and events he hoped he had buried were resurrected. He had become close to Sylvia and to the boy. He loved them both. He couldn't stand to think of the degradation she had been through with Morgan. The idea of Morgan laying a finger on William horrified him. It must be prevented, and he must see to it.

Three nights later. Morgan was at home in his Finchley mansion, half asleep, on the first floor, alone in his bed. He heard a noise. A shadow passed across his half-closed eyes.

A lighted cannister dropped from the air onto the duvet which covered the lower half of his torso. His pyjama jacket was quickly set alight and the flames spread. Furiously he shoved aside the covering. But the cannister was immediately followed by a liquid, sprayed onto him from a point in the room. His body was doused all over. The flames spread more rapidly, increasing in intensity. He screamed out. No one there to help. The shadow wasn't concerned to rescue him. The shadow was too busy spraying more of the liquid onto him. His pyjamas were blazing, his flesh scorched, the pain unbearable.

The bed rapidly heated up. Jim Morgan got caught up in a tangle of flaming duvet and sheets. The fire spread, and the intruder ran from the bedroom and escaped through an open window in the hall, jumping down and onto a canvas which had been strategically rigged below to break the fall. Morgan's bed was now white hot. The carpet under the bed burst into flames.

Sometime after, the flaming pyre, with its charred and twisted occupant, crashed through the blazing floorboards weakened by the fire, and into the room below, spreading the inferno to the lower part of the mansion.

That night, Morgan's home burnt down. The fire crew had been unable to do any more than to stop the conflagration from spreading across the shrubbery and ravaging the summer house. Late on the following day, when the heat had abated sufficiently for the wreckage to be examined, Morgan's remains were found lying in a pool of black tarry substance.

The night after the fire, Sylvia and William had gone to visit a friend. Alone in his flat, Danny Silver, alias Adam Steele, the singer, undid its clasp and opened up a scrapbook which he had kept for years, hidden away in a battered brown leather satchel, a reminder of his school days. He flicked through the pages until he came to an article from a colour magazine dated March 20th, 1947. There was a photo of a young boy. He had not read this piece in a long time. As he read the article slowly to himself, it took on a new significance.

"A six-year-old boy escaped unharmed in Moss Side, Manchester, from a fire he had set on Tuesday as revenge for being punished by his grandpa," police and local firemen said. "Daniel Silver had run away and survived the flames, after he used a lighter to set the drapes on fire in the home of Micky Silver, his paternal grandfather. Mr Silver suffered third degree burns to sixty percent of the body, but should survive the terrible ordeal."

"It's about revenge," a source who knew the boy well, was quoted as saying. "What's awful is that Danny is only six."

The youngster had prank phoned 999 and told the police that his grandpa was dead or seriously ill. To punish the child, his grandfather had forbidden him playing with his pet rabbit and had locked it up in the outside lavatory. He had also forbidden the boy from going to the cinema with his two older mates. But they ran out and went to the pictures anyway.

As they left the house, Daniel told his friends that he was going to burn the house down and kill his granddad, because the old man had tortured his pet. His uncle Monty Spiro, told reporters, "When he was two, the baby played with matches."

A friend of the family said that little Danny frequently told his grandpa he would burn the house down if he didn't get his way.

Danny Silver finished reading the article. He looked at the photo. It was a picture of a good-looking child of six, the colour image showed curly blonde hair. But the eyes were the most distinctive. Bright blue eyes, the left one with a distinct greenish cast.

Queen Victoria's Ghost

It was while staying at Bleak House in Broadstairs that Polly started to believe in ghosts. She'd previously been a fierce non-believer, for at that time Polly was a confirmed atheist, not in the least bit spiritual. Indeed, one of her nicknames was 'Practical Pol'.

To her, religion was fairy stories, and stuff like astrology, faith healing, ghosts and ghouls, were irrational fodder for "airy fairy folk", as she called them. Practical Pol was down to earth, inhabiting a solid world, with no room for doubt about a possible life after death. There wasn't one, she claimed.

Esther, her best friend, was the opposite. Indeed, they were different in many ways, for Polly, at thirty-four was tall and dainty and extremely pretty, while Esther, in her mid-fifties was a mere five foot and overweight, her ruddy complexion plastered with make-up, her hair a bright dyed blonde, her figure blousy and inelegant. But they were great buddies and had once wowed people, at a fancy-dress party, suitably dressed as 'PollyEsther'!

Polly worked for a solicitor, Esther was a successful actress, now mostly "resting". Despite their differences they often hung out together, as Esther brought a degree of entertainment into Polly's otherwise matter-of-fact life, while Practical Pol helped Esther with her financial affairs, which, without Polly's help, would have remained in a ramshackle state.

One winter evening, the two friends were staying at St Mary's Cliffe, a large and partly derelict house in Alderley Edge, near Manchester. Over a rather wine-soaked dinner, Esther had raised the subject of ghosts. Apparently, the house was haunted by child ghosts. Esther believed this. Her friend, Mary, an athletic looking brunette of forty-two, who lived in an apartment on the ground floor, claimed to have seen the ghost of a young boy one night, through the glass door into the hallway.

"Mind you, her son, Peter, might have got up from his bed to go to the loo," Esther said. But Esther preferred to believe the ghost interpretation.

"A local author, I can't think of his name, has written a book about the children haunting the house, so it must be true," she told Polly.

A few weeks later they arranged a gathering at St Mary's Cliffe, determined to go into the derelict area, in the dead of night, and hoping to experience the ghosts for themselves.

"They are only the spirits of children, there will be no harm," claimed Esther.

So, Mary, Esther and Polly, together with friends, David and Anthony, (both accountants in their mid-forties, but just going along with the ladies for a giggle), crept stealthily into the uninhabited quarters of the house. They all carried torches which lit up the recesses of the cobweb-covered rooms, casting deep shadows across dusty floors, and beaming thin paths of light up the walls. Sometimes faces would be illuminated, but it was merely their own faces. They saw no ghosts; they heard no children sounds. After an hour of stalking around in the increasingly cold and dank rooms, the men were totally bored.

"I'm off, back for another drink," said Anthony.

"Come on, girls, there are no ghosts here," whispered David.

And they both turned and began to make their way to the door leading back to Mary's flat.

"I don't want to be here without the men," said Mary.

"It's okay," said Practical Pol, there's nothing to be afraid of, I'm sure."

Esther was equally sure she had just felt a cold chill over her skin, though she said nothing, but she and Mary joined the men on their way out. Polly decided that another glass of Merlot would be a good idea. So, they all went back to Mary's lounge where they had a few more glasses before turning in for the rest of the night.

The next morning, at breakfast, Esther, joined the others late, looking dishevelled and distraught, her pasty skin without make-up, her hair transformed from its vibrant blond to ashen grey.

"Are you alright?" said Practical Pol. "You look awful."

"I had the most frightening night. A ghost got into my bed!" Esther appeared to be almost broken, shivering in distress.

"Whaaaat?" said Anthony and David, almost in unison. "You are having us on."

Mary looked aghast at the others. Polly put her arm round Esther, who was weeping now. She spluttered out her story.

"I'd gone to bed and was nearly asleep. I felt cold before, in the derelict rooms. I never told you, but I did feel a horrible coldness there."

The others continued to stare at her, transfixed by the story she told.

"Then I felt the cold again, only this time, it was accompanied by a sound, and a damp breeze. It got into bed with me. I tell you, the cover turned back and something moist and cold slid next to me and lay against me. I must have blacked out, because I don't remember anything else.

When I woke everything seemed normal, everything that is except me! Look at me, look at the state I am in!'"

Esther wept and shivered. Had she gone mad? Maybe this was all an act! Was she really having them on, as the men had said? Polly knew that Esther was inclined to over-dramatise her life and sometimes liked to use her acting skills to play practical jokes. But Esther seemed genuinely frightened out of her skin, and the grey hair seemed visible evidence of the ordeal she had suffered the night before.

They were all due to depart that afternoon, and the two other ladies helped Esther get her things together. A while later, as they left St Mary's Cliffe, Polly noticed that her friend had uncharacteristically tucked her hair into a large, floppy hat. On the train back to London, Polly realised that Esther had calmed down. She was even eating a chicken sandwich, most heartily. Then she began to smile, then a cheesy grin, and finally she broke into a giggle. Esther removed her hat, and her bright blonde hair tumbled down onto her ample shoulders. Polly could hardly believe this second transformation in her friend.

"I really had you all going didn't I," cackled Esther. "Oh, it was beautiful to see you all. You really believed my ghost story, didn't you?"

"You wicked woman," replied Practical Pol, but couldn't help laughing. Hadn't Esther's practical joke, simply confirmed Polly's own scepticism about ghosts? There were no ghosts. She'd been right all along.

Fast forward some months later, to Bleak House, overlooking the famed Viking Bay in Broadstairs, and where Charles Dickens had written some of *David Copperfield*. Bleak House was the iconic building in the town, and pictures of it were in almost every pub, wine bar, café and restaurant in the area.

Polly had been invited for the Easter holiday to stay with the owners, who she and Esther had met at a party in London. She had asked the owners if they were happy for her to bring her best friend Esther, and they had graciously agreed, especially as they had been impressed by Esther's theatrical background. The friends had read a Broadstairs guidebook and were fascinated by Bleak House and its relics of a past age. The book described an abundance of memorabilia related to the author; the room where Dickens wrote, his desk and chair, the wonderful sea views from his "airy nest" as he'd called it. Even more fascinating to Polly and Esther was the account of the bedroom next door to Dickens's room, which contained a brass bed, formerly housed at the Bull Inn in Rochester, in which Queen Victoria had slept as a young girl. Practical Pol found herself compelled to research the history of the brass bed. Sometime after sleeping in the bed at the Bull in Rochester, the young queen had it transported to the Palace. She and Albert, once they were married, (if not before), slept in it frequently. Many years later Queen Victoria's bed was purchased at auction by previous owners of Bleak House. Polly was to sleep in this bed during her stay. She tingled at the thought.

Finally, the two friends had been told of the cellars which contained a number of separate chambers, each housing waxworks and other displays illustrating the local smuggling trade of the early and middle eighteenth century. There were still tunnels underneath Bleak House connected with this traffic. Polly felt a weird, almost otherworldly feeling when she visited this part of the property.

Polly couldn't wait until she was tucked up in Queen Victoria's bed and so that night, at just ten o'clock, and after a hearty meal with Esther and her hosts, and rather too much red wine, she turned in and eventually fell into a half sleep. Perhaps it was the cheese course at dinner that disturbed her, but she found it hard to remain asleep, half dozing, half awake, and thinking of the strange effigies of the old-time smugglers in that creepy cellar two floors beneath where she lay.

She heard a clock chime, one o' clock, and then a rustling sound near the bed. In the gloom she thought she saw something, or was it somebody? Polly shuddered, and drew the blanket over her. What was it? She forced herself to peer over the edge of her covers. She couldn't believe what she saw. The figure stood at the side of the bed. Short and robust of stature, dressed all in black except for a white cap. Surely not? But to the terrified, yet fascinated Polly, there was no mistaking the identity of the wraith-like creature at the bedside. It was the ghost of Queen Victoria, near the end of her long reign. Her beloved Albert's sudden death in 1861 had devastated the queen and plunged her into the mourning black from which she would never emerge. And so, the spirit wore a sort of widow's uniform that had become her trademark, a full-skirted black gown with a bodice that buttoned down the front and completed with the ubiquitous white cap that would be forever associated with the queen. The figure was gazing longingly at the bed but didn't seem to be aware of its occupant.

Polly who had never believed in ghosts, found herself quite calm in the presence of this extraordinary vision. But she felt no threat, and the longer the ghost stood there the more Practical Pol felt reassured.

It was if the queen was concentrating deeply, remembering her past, wanting to recapture something, or perhaps somebody lost to her. The ghost just stood there and gazed sadly, most sadly at the bed. Polly couldn't quite believe her own sentiments, for she felt sorry for this dumpy, old, yet still most regal personage. Polly experienced no fear, no panic, just wonder and sadness. Time passed, nothing else happened, just the two of them, Polly under the covers peering out to look at the ghost of Queen Victoria, the spirit, in a trance, looking at the brass bed. Polly felt drowsiness overcome her, and fell into a deep sleep. Queen Victoria's ghost stood a while longer then gradually walked away. It was as if she wanted to stay there forever but hadn't the strength to do so.

Polly had been privileged to witness the ghost of Queen Victoria trying to relive some of those precious moments in bed with the husband she had worshipped. As for Practical Pol, she now believed in ghosts. She seriously believed in ghosts!

The following morning, Polly went to the bedroom next to hers to suggest that she and Esther could breakfast together. A quick knock on the door. Silence. "Esther, are you awake? I have something really weird to tell you about last night. You have been right all the time. I'll tell you over breakfast." Still silence. "Esther, I'm coming in."

The door was unlocked, and Practical Pol entered. She heard the shower going full pelt in the en suite. Esther was obviously getting herself ready, and was unable to hear the door knocks.

As she walked into the bedroom Polly's attention was drawn to various items that gave the lie to her newly found belief in ghosts. For there, thrown over the armchair, was an old black costume dress of Victorian style, a grey wig and a white cap, and on the dressing table she noticed several jars of special make-up. Esther had fooled her again!

Animal Tragic

Winston Stanley, a slight, balding, most nervous man, in his late fifties. His Adam's apple stuck out. He walked with a stoop. Winston lived alone, in an untidy house in north London. He had withdrawn into solitude since his wife had left him for a younger man. He had not lived solo since before his marriage, and was incapable of looking after himself. He ate sporadically, junk food, often past its use-by date, drank heavily, and found it difficult to sleep. In short, Winston Stanley was a wreck. These days, he struggled to concentrate on his work. He kept his occupation a secret.

Morning, still in his dressing gown. A knock on the front door. It was the postman with a long parcel. Winston wasn't expecting a delivery, but signed for it, intrigued to discover the contents. He didn't wait to leave the hallway, and tore hurriedly at the wrapper once the postman had departed. There was a nice box inside, about fifty-five centimetres long and twenty-two centimetres square. It was duck egg blue, made from rigid cardboard.

He opened the box. Inside, a beautiful glass bottle, coffin shaped, containing a colourless liquid, and an item that disturbed Winston when he recognised the piece of the animal. He held the bottle to the light in his scraggy hands, his thin fingers wrapping around its shape. He examined the contents. It was the hairy brown tail of a dog, carefully placed inside the gorgeous container. Though the vessel was much larger, the elegance of its design reminded him of a sophisticated cosmetics product, one of those chic brands advertised on television. He could rarely afford to buy such delights for his wife, and now she had deserted him. He noticed a piece of art paper with some writing.

"Remember, a doggy is not just for Christmas."

Winston shuddered in horror at this sinister invasion. In disgust he thrust aside the box, the bottle, wrapper and note. Agitated, he turned from the hallway, reeling towards his lounge. He attacked the whisky bottle left open on a chair, handy for when he watched television alone at night. He gulped one glassful, poured a second, and drank more slowly, imagining the dog's tail. He could still picture the end of the tail, severed from the rest of the animal. It was a long tail. It must have been a large dog. Winston's mind began to ask questions.

Who sent this abomination, and why? Should I tell the police? What would happen next?

He sat there, several long minutes, not knowing what to do. In sudden recollection, the possible origin of the present dawned. He felt faint at the thought, and rapidly started from his seat. Manically, he leafed through a stack of newspapers, trying to find something he'd read. When he found the article he sank back into his chair, moaning as he realised that this gift might only be the beginning. Eventually he managed to compose himself. He dressed, then shoved the package and its disturbing contents inside the understairs cupboard. He phoned the people at work. He was too upset to go in.

Winston found it hard to banish from his thoughts the beautiful bottle and its ugly contents. He started to watch a film. He was a bit of a movie buff and had a state-of-the-art television and DVD player. But he was unable to concentrate. The curly brown tail played on his mind. His stomach churned. The whisky didn't help.

Winston was a poor sleeper. That night was much worse, for he couldn't forget the image of the canine tail, curled around inside the jar, like some malevolent snake. The container had somehow escaped from the cupboard and was lying on his bed. In his twisted mind the beautiful bottle had stretched to the size of a coffin. It kept expanding. The hairy brown tail inside grew, and grew more hideous, until it burst open the glass. Gallons of liquid spilled out and ran towards him. The tail, transformed into a writhing creature, wriggled onto his throat, grasping and throttling him. He was gasping for air; the fluid ran freely over him. He nearly went under. He was drowning in the formalin, for he now recognised the strong, pungent, chemical smell, which got up his nose and stung his eyes.

The next morning Winston lay shivering in his bed. The front doorbell rang. He willed himself to get up, and managed to force his skinny legs down the stairs. As he turned the central heating full on, he noticed the clock on the wall by the front door – the same time as yesterday's postal delivery.

"Mornin' again, sir," said the postman. "Nice mornin' too, sir. Another parcel. Sign 'ere please."

The postman handed him the parcel. It was smaller and more square than yesterday's. Winston checked the name and address on the dark green wrapping and on the docket. Sure enough, the parcel was for him. Pulling himself together he signed, and muttered his thanks. He closed the front door and took the package into his lounge. He was in no hurry to open it. Instead, he placed it on the coffee table and stood staring. Then he picked it up and shook it. He could hear a sloshing around inside. He almost dropped the parcel in fright.

"Oh no, it's another one," he cried aloud in anguish. Winston was intensely distressed.

What shall I do? What shall I do? I have to open it. I must see. I must!

Winston took a knife and flicked at the edges of the green wrapping paper. He soon saw another nice box. It was duck egg blue, like the first. He opened it. A large round jar

133

lay before him. Its design reminded him of an expensive bottle of perfume. He recoiled from what he saw inside. The severed head of a cat, floating around, and he was certain of this, preserved, just to horrify him. Each pair of the cat's eyelids had been sewn together. He slumped down into his armchair. There was a note.

"Another little gift for you, because I know you love all of God's creatures."

Winston froze into his seat and fell into a stupor.

He must have lain there several hours, but was woken by the sound of a car drawing up to the front of the house. Footsteps, and then the sound of something being placed at the door. Moments later the vehicle drove off. Winston was exhausted, emotionally drained, and physically weakened by fear. Had someone come for him? What would he find at his front entrance? He didn't want to look, but knew he needed to find out the worst. He already suspected there would be another gift waiting for him. He remembered the newspaper article reporting a similar pattern of events, some months before. There had been gruesome photographs.

It was dark, and as he opened his front door, the glare of a large torch perched on top of a parcel shone directly into his eyes. Someone had stuck text onto the light end of the torch so that a message would be projected when the torch was switched on. Words played over his face, the top half of his torso and onto the wall behind him. Winston moved away and looked. He read the image.

"A rat for a rat."

Winston grabbed the parcel and the torch, and bundled them inside the house. He flung the torch down on the floor where it continued to play out its message, distorted by the angle of its projected light onto a corner of the hallway. Winston tore at the package. Another duck egg blue box, another exquisite clear glass container. Inside a large rat floated in formalin. Another message written on fine art paper.

"Did you know, that according to scientists, this little creature shares many of your genes?" He sobbed and shook. *When would this end? What was next?*

He realised that there would be more to come, that some malevolent force was seeking retribution.

"Hello," his thin voice faltered, "this is Winston Stanley. Please, I must speak to someone." He had telephoned the local police station directly.

"Yes, I must report a series of grotesque presents which I have been receiving. Please send someone over here as soon as possible."

The person at the other end recognised that Winston Stanley was terrified and noted the address.

"Calm yourself, sir. An officer will be with you in ten minutes."

A while later, a ring at the bell. Winston, who had been drinking from a newly-opened whisky bottle, shambled to the door, and the uniformed officer entered. Within fifteen minutes Winston had recounted the frightening events, shown the "gifts" and answered some questions. Yes, he lived alone, he was head of a science project at a local laboratory. No, he didn't know who might have sent the parcels. The policeman wasn't sympathetic.

This chap is drunk. He is a total mess.

Had the officer been more thorough, had he probed more deeply, facts would have emerged which should have pointed the finger more clearly at who might be responsible for the incidents that so deeply troubled Winston Stanley. And in his confused and severely weakened state, Winston omitted two most important pieces of information. He failed to mention the true nature of his scientific work, or the newspaper article that so obsessed him.

The policeman didn't say it, but he wondered if the gifts were just some sick practical joke, albeit from someone who had gone to lots of trouble and a degree of expense. Perhaps Winston's ex-wife still bore some kind of grudge? He soon departed, promising to discuss with colleagues "these incidents". He would be in touch. Meanwhile he advised Winston to get a good night's sleep, try to take things easy, lay off the bottle.

Winston, still unable to return to work. A fevered, stick insect of a man, he was sweating heavily, burning up. He was drinking even more, sleeping fitfully, hardly eating, and suffering from muscle spasms, desperately clutching at his body and shrieking erratically. His clothing stuck to him, so he tore it off and shuffled around in his underwear. The house stank from rotting food and his unclean body. Several days passed. Some new, more disturbing, presents had appeared at his porch on the same day, Christmas Eve.

They were animal parts, but unlike the other gifts, these were from human animals. A man's ear, a section of a female hand with four fingers, one with a wedding band, and finally a human foot. These offerings were not presented in beautiful glass bottles, but were separate bundles of rags, each one containing its grotesque deposit. Three gifts, Christmas. A bell rang in his jangled brain. Wise men bearing gold, frankincense and myrrh. There was only one note for the three human bits.

"Winston Stanley, most unmanly, kills little animals."

Christmas night. The house, over-heated, filthy with grime and waste. Blown light bulbs. Emaciated figure on a ladder at the top of his stairs, naked except for thin underpants. Blotchy yellowed skin, drips sweat. Torch, to give him

136

light, projects its rat message up the stairway. He reaches out and with difficulty throws a length of rope over the fake oak beam that runs above the stair well. He dismounts and replaces the ladder with a chair on which he then stands and ties the rope around his scrawny neck.

Winston Stanley kicks away the chair and plummets down, into the void, breaking his neck as the weight of his body forces the rope to snap tight. The rat word shines across his dangling wet torso. He does not die immediately. Had he not been so skinny, a bag of bones, he would have suffered less.

Double Death

Harry Boy and Joey Boy had three things in common. The first was that they were brothers. Secondly, they were both known as 'Boy'. But they shared something else, and this was most unusual. For the brothers both died on the same day.

The 'Boy' thing was just one of those names of affection that Jewish parents sometimes gave their children back then, in the nineteen-thirties and forties, though both brothers felt it was sometimes employed to put them in their place. A few months before Harry Boy's bar mitzvah, and when they had seen their first Hollywood crime movies, they began to get a buzz from being addressed as Harry Boy and Joey Boy.

"I like my name now. I feel like a gangster in those Mafia films," Joey Boy remarked one morning as they got dressed for breakfast. "They had names a bit like ours. Although theirs were more colourful, like 'Louis the Lip' and 'Bugsy Segal'. We are different from the other kids, and our names are special."

"Me too," said Harry Boy. "I want to be like Baby Face Nelson." He went over to his bedside and pulled out a toy Thompson sub machine gun from under his bed. He knew all the slang names for his weapon, and delighted in referring to it by each of them in turn. So at various times it had become his 'Chicago Piano', or his 'Trench Broom'. On occasion it was dubbed the 'Chicago Typewriter'. At other times it was 'Trench Sweeper.' But 'Tommy Gun' was his favourite name.

Harry Boy stepped away from the bed and fired his weapon straight at his brother. It made a sharp rat-at-tat sound.

"Missed me, you punk. You don't get Spats Columbo

138

that easy," Joey responded, creasing his face into an aggressive leer. "You bedda come across with the dough, or I'll get the guys to bury you in cement."

"Yeh, you and who's army?" Harry was more powerfully built than his brother and would take no lip from him, even though they were just horsing around in a game of gangster make-believe.

They didn't look like brothers. Harry was built like a cube. Short and squat, everything about him was chunky. Square jaw on a flat face, the features hardly sticking out at all, the hair slicked and combed flat, square shoulders, thick arms, stumpy fat legs. He did have a winning smile, though, which displayed a set of clear white, perfect teeth. Harry was a charmer, when he wanted to be, and as he grew up, despite his bulk he would attract many young ladies, for he exuded energy and success.

Joey was tall and gangly, sometimes nicknamed by the street kids, 'Joey Beanstalk'. His short, curly mop top was invariably unruly. His aquiline nose, ears stuck out, thick lips and uneven teeth did him no favours. No one would call him an attractive boy, and as he grew up he developed into even less of a looker.

Harry Boy was also a father. He had married Helen Cohen from the neighbourhood, and their son, Howard, was a cheeky eight-year-old, who liked to pee in the garden to see what it would do to the flowers. I still have an old eight-millimetre movie I shot of Howard, taking out his little circumcised pecker to wee on the daffodils.

Joey was still unmarried, mostly out of work, and relying on handouts from his mother, or the money he could earn working on the street markets for his uncle Mo.

"Another one sold, over there, to the bloke with the silver hair," he called out from inside the East End market

139

stall, as he handed out the cheap canteen of cutlery to a florid-faced geezer in a grubby brown jacket.

Joey liked the gaffs, one of the few places where he seemed to come alive with an energy normally reserved for sleeping. When he wasn't working the gaffs, playing stud poker, or blackjack, Joey stayed in bed. Not so, Harry Boy, Mr Dynamic. He was everywhere. "Fingers in pies, cakes and biscuits," his father Abe would say.

"Why can't Joey Boy be more like Harry?" he moaned to Dolly. "Tell me that my little lockshen pudding."

"I'll give you lockshen pudding," his wife sneered. The marriage had been on the rocks for over twenty years. Abe had an active libido, Dolly believed that sex was for having babies, and her two were enough. So Abe had a buxom mistress, Becky Daniels, and enjoyed "giving her a feel" as he boasted to his friends. For her part, Dolly felt contempt. But she endured, for the children.

She reminded her husband.

"When Harry came out, he was smiling when I first held him. He must have liked what he saw, and has made the most of it. Joey was scowling and yelling from the start. And you know that he resents being the second son. He is just jealous and eats himself up with envy. I wish it was different with him, but I am afraid it might be too late. He needs a good woman to give him some purpose in his life."

"Yes? Who do you think will put up with him then? He's a lost cause if you ask me."

"Not completely," responded Dolly. "He has a real talent on the gaffs. He can sell. That's what he should try to do."

"He only likes the gaffs cos he can put his fingers in the till. I've seen him do it." On a few occasions, when Abe had helped Mo out on the markets, he'd been disturbed to see Joey helping himself to the odd tenner from the money box at the back of the square trestle top, inside which the five market boys worked their routines. He had kept schtum though. Later on, Abe became aware that Joey was stealing money from his brother's wallet. He'd caught him lifting the wallet from Harry's jacket and pinching some of the paper stuff and some loose change. Once again though, the father hadn't breathed a word.

Harry Boy, the ubiquitous Mr Dynamic, never needed handouts. At seventeen he got in with a young American from an air force base, and organised some kind of concession to sell Havana cigars to his friends' parents. Word spread, and soon many of the men in the local Jewish community were among his customers. This helped to put him through college, where he made lots of contacts among the student population. He had a plan to make real money from the kids who were keen to find excitement after the college bars closed.

In his mid-twenties, Harry opened a club for students from the local colleges. He was able to do a deal with the owners of a disco in Whitechapel town centre. Costas, and his English wife Margaret, had run the club, but lost their drinks' licence. Business had dwindled, and so when Harry Boy walked in, soon after the licence had been renewed, they were pleased with his business proposition.

"I can bring in a hundred and fifty students two nights a week, during college terms. I will take the door money, you take the bar money, what do you say?"

Costas and Margaret conferred, and soon after, Costas shook hands with the young entrepreneur.

"You a young man, but you got a lotta confidence."

"Too true," replied Harry Boy. "Now I need two weeks to promote the club nights. We will do a disco on Wednesdays, and for Thursdays I will book groups. And when they are not playing, my deejay will play disco music. Okay?"

"Very good, I will make some food for the kids to go with their drinking. It's a requirement of the licence. They will have to pay for the food."

"That's good," said Harry Boy. "I will let them know the entrance and food prices in my handouts, and also the price for a pint of beer. Most of them will want beer you know."

The two nights were a raving success, and Harry coined it. He made himself over a hundred quid a night, though things died down dramatically during the student vacations. He publicised the club nights on a regular weekly basis to keep up the momentum, and make sure business picked up quickly at the beginning of each new term.

During the mid to late sixties, Harry became aware of changes in the music scene. Popular music was being influenced by new performers and songwriters, and becoming more diverse and musically challenging. Harry felt he knew what the kids wanted from their music, and he wanted a piece of this business. He signed up a bunch of guys from Manchester, who played heavier electric guitar numbers with a more rebellious feel. He renamed them 'The Blades', and with money saved from the students' club nights he brought them to London and quickly launched them onto the developing rock scene. Their first single, *Revolution Row*, was a massive hit and the band quickly built up a huge popular following, released an album, played at big concert venues, toured Europe, Japan and America, and appeared on several prestigious television shows. Harry Boy grew very rich.

Joey grew despondent. He was getting nowhere in life. His envy of his brother consumed him. Before Harry had met Helen, he was engaged to Susan, a very beautiful girl from the neighbourhood. She was raven-haired and voluptuous, and Joey coveted her for himself. So he made up a story that Harry had stayed overnight at Rachel's, one of the other girls they hung out with. The story was false, but Susan had a suspicious mind, and it poisoned her against Harry, and for a while she went with Joey, then dumped him as more of their crowd took Harry's side in the matter. But because Susan had been with the younger brother, Harry didn't want to know her anymore. Soon after, he met Helen, and they were married within a few months.

Because of his envious behaviour, Joey was ostracised by most of the community. He went downhill, smoking more and more, drinking heavily, taking cocktails of drugs, sleeping late, talking to himself, falling apart. He had lost most of his hair by the time he was thirty. At thirty-one, Harry was a millionaire, married, with a son. Joey, younger by a year, was an unsuccessful gambler, a nebbish.

"If only I could win big," Joey said aloud one morning, as he looked in the mirror at his pale and emaciated appearance. "I need a chance, just one."

The chance never came. Joey Boy's health deteriorated dramatically. He was diagnosed with cancer of the liver and eventually taken into hospital.

Harry Boy visited his brother. Their boyhood games had been tinged with a rivalry that had grown increasingly bitter. As Harry had prospered, and Joey became a failure and then lied that his brother had slept with Rachel, this antagonism between the two boys had worsened. Harry was ashamed of his brother, felt revulsion for him, while Joey's envy was like a worm nibbling away inside his guts.

It was difficult for Harry to bring himself to go to see Joey, when what he really wanted was to have nothing to do with him, to disown him. But his brother owed him money and he was determined to make one last effort to retrieve the debt. Besides he couldn't resist lauding it over his sorry sibling.

"So, Joey, how's the chopped liver?" Harry leered at the bedridden form.

"Still your favourite sandwich?"

Joey scowled.

"Piss off…"

Harry Boy sat down.

"At least I can piss straight. Look at you, skin and bones. How could you let yourself get like this? Where's your self-respect? And what about the three hundred you owe me?"

Harry had lent his brother three ton. Two years later, Joey still owed.

"I'll leave it you in my will."

"You don't have it! I will have to write it off, just like I wrote you off years ago."

Harry got up from his chair, wheeled round and left. He couldn't stand to see his brother. What a schlemiel! The older brother felt shame that this piece of garbage was a member of his family. He also felt guilt that he'd become so alienated from his own flesh and blood. So he had to get out of the place. It was the last the brothers were to see of each other.

Early in the morning of the day when Joey Boy wheezed out his final few breaths, Harry had caught a plane to California, where The Blades were performing a concert in a large open-air venue. That night he was on stage as they belted out their opening set, under the bright, flashing stage lights and sweaty atmosphere. It was hot and muggy, the security was seriously shambolic, and the huge crowd contained members of Hell's Angels who'd biked in and had been drinking heavily.

Without warning, a violent-looking toughie, gun in hand, elbowed his way towards the stage and took aim at Lee James, the iconic Blades frontman. Lee was unaware, high on speed, and deep into his screaming vocal, swerving his lithe body to the crashing beat. The shot rang out. Lee was in the air, leaping to the groove.

Behind him Mr Dynamic felt the hot plug of metal from the .45 calibre bullet searing into him. It was like dynamite exploding inside his shirt. The bullet tore into the heart. He collapsed on stage. Harry Boy's life's performance had been cut short. No more rock n' roll!

On the same night that Harry was shot, back across the pond, my mother, was travelling to London on the eight twenty-five evening train from Leicester. I met her at St. Pancras station. She told me that she'd just seen Harry Boy on the train, that night, the night he died. I was incredulous. "How can that be? He is in the States, at a concert for The Blades, his rock group."

"I was almost asleep in the carriage," she said. "I had my head laying back against the seat. Then I felt a drip on my forehead and heard the drip, dripping of water from somewhere in the carriage. I looked up. It was falling from the condensation on the roof of the train. And then I saw him, I saw Harry Boy. You know how he was always grinning, that self-satisfied grin of his. 'Mr Smug' I would call him. Well, this time he wasn't grinning. But there he was, his head was anyway, I didn't see any more of him. There was no body, just his head perched on the luggage rack, squashed into the space between two attaché cases. He looked disappointed is all I can say about his expression."

When I left Mother, I really didn't know what to think. My mum is normally sceptical about the existence of spirits. "All that ghosts and ghoulies stuff. It's a load of old twaddle," she would say. "Mind you, I do like a good horror film."

Near midnight, the same evening, the phone was ringing as I got home from Mum's apartment in Hampstead. I heard it as I opened the front door. Mum's account of Harry Boy's ghost was still playing on my mind. Like my mum, I didn't believe in out-of-body experiences, but Mother had seemed so sure about what she had witnessed. I rushed to the phone, picked it up and spoke into the mouthpiece.

"Hello, Philip here." I could just make out a faint whisper at the other end of the line.

"Phil, it's your aunty Dolly. My poor Joey Boy just passed away in the hospital, and Harry has been shot dead in America. Two terrible phone calls to me. Both my boys, gone on the same day. Now I really am on my own. Where is God?"

The voice faltered. I heard her crying. She had lived alone for two years, after Abe had died.

"Philip, why did this happen to me?"

I had no reply for her. I just muttered a cliché, about how sorry I was for her loss, and wished her long life. But I also knew of the hostility between the two sons, and was aware that Dolly knew this.

"Philip, I will tell you the day of the funeral as soon as it's been arranged," she gasped. She sobbed, could barely continue talking. She was totally distraught, and what she said next, well, I wasn't sure if she was in full possession of her faculties.

"My two sons," she wailed, "Harry Boy and my Joey Boy. I will speak to the rabbi. Our family has been members of the shul, since before I can remember. We have paid out loads of gelt, all these years. So I will talk with Rabbi Feltz. I am sure he will agree. I will ask him to arrange it so that my boys are buried, side by side, in one double coffin, their hands clasped together! Maybe I haven't been such a good mother, but I will make sure that my sons are reconciled in death."

The shul had many arcane rituals, but I had never heard of such a burial arrangement and was pretty sure the rabbi wouldn't allow this. But then again, who knows? For the right money.

Horror Hammer

Many of the attendees travelled a fair distance to the event. Some hoped to pick up a bargain at the auction, which was being held at the Frimlington Palace Hotel, near Maidstone. Others just came to watch.

Albert Higgins and Colin Mason came to buy. They were among the crowd in the hotel reception area, just inside the entrance. This space was set out to provide tea, coffee and snacks, prior to the commencement of the proceedings, which were to be held in the smaller of the hotel's two conference rooms. Many of those who were coming in could be seen holding their blue and yellow catalogues, giving details of the properties for auction. The catalogue listed the properties, all of them residential: houses and flats. There were details of the accommodation, and photographs of the exterior of each of the lots. But it was a series of photographs from police files that had drawn many of the audience to the event. For underneath the main image of each property were grotesque pictures of what had happened to the residents, or in some instances, an unfortunate visitor to the premises.

The hotel reception area was specially furnished with some tables where a few of the auction team from John Pilgrim and Sons were sitting, filling out details of those who intended to bid in the auction. Three specialist companies had stands in a corner of the area. These were people who helped to provide information on the properties for the due diligence of prospective purchasers. They also specialised in mortgages and legal services.

Albert Higgins, a portly man of forty-three with blotchy, reddish skin, motioned to his business partner to help carry their coffee and sandwiches.

"There won't be a huge attendance. Not for what they

are auctioning today. I mean, let's face it, there aren't that many of us around."

"Just as well," Colin replied. "The fewer there are to bid, the more chance we have to pick up something cheap." Colin Mason, a builder by trade, was six foot two inches, lanky and pasty faced. He spoke from the side of his mouth, giving the impression that his lips were slightly crooked.

Nevertheless, when they eventually proceeded through the reception area and into the conference room, they were surprised to see so many there. Albert and Colin sat on a couple of chairs near the stage. Albert counted the numbers in the rows, multiplied that figure by the number of rows, and worked out an approximate total. He reckoned over one hundred and fifty people were present in the audience. John Pilgrim and Sons had established that there would be far less attendance than for a normal property auction, and therefore the much larger, main conference hall, would not be required.

Imagine an outsider, a stranger to this type of property auction, suddenly landing inside the conference room. I am willing to bet good money that this person would have soon noticed that the audience contained a large number of weirdos. The more our stranger looked and listened, the more it might seem that some of those present had walked off the set of a horror movie. Once the outsider realised the true nature of what was being auctioned, it would become clear that many of the intending bidders were motivated not just by the need to make a profit from their purchase, but by a fetish for the macabre and the gruesome. Indeed, those who just came to look could frequently be seen pointing to the appalling photographs in the catalogue, muttering to their neighbour in approval at some image of a severed limb or a lacerated neck. They reminded one of the good citizens of Paris during the French revolution, who got their kicks by watching Madame La Guillotine perform her duties, severing the heads of the aristocracy from their bodies.

The small conference room was laid out with the usual trappings for a property auction. A large blue and yellow banner, hanging from the ceiling over the stage, proudly displayed the logo of the auction house, 'John Pilgrim and Sons, Auctioneers, for over one hundred years'. There was a long trestle table on the stage, at which sat a man and a woman who would record the bids. A lectern had been positioned at the front of the platform, behind which stood the auctioneer, Dominic Pilgrim, the great grandson of the company's founder. To the right of him could be seen a television camera, the cameraman already in place, taking shots as the room filled up.

Dominic was in his middle fifties, smartly dressed with a red flower in his button hole. A matching red handkerchief peeked out from the top pocket of his neatly-tailored jacket. He had a full head of iron-grey hair, distinguished features, and an erect, slightly military posture. He looked well fed, fit and above all, moneyed. Then, on a signal from a colleague in the room, he motioned for those present to come to order. He spoke with authority. He'd been conducting auctions for the best part of thirty years.

"Ladies and gentlemen. It is good to see you all here. Thank you for showing such interest in today's auction of residential property with a difference." He pointed to a large screen to his left.

"The main photo of each property will be displayed here, as it comes up for auction. When people bid, the bid price will be displayed at the top of the screen."

He then explained further how he would conduct the event, and the requirements placed on any purchaser for a ten percent deposit on the day. He also indicated that, ideally, bidders should have conducted their own research into any property they wished to purchase, prior to the auction. They should also have ensured, if their final bid was successful, that they had their funds in place to meet the agreed purchase price.

"By the way, we are being filmed today for the television programme, *Horror Homes Under the Hammer*. The camera you see on my right will record today's proceedings for the television show. So if any of you are here with someone who you shouldn't be seen with, you had better duck down, away from the lens!"

The audience laughed; Dominic Pilgrim smiled. Dominic Pilgrim was a bit of an entertainer.

"Okay, let's begin. Lot Thirty-eight. This is number 42 Coronation Drive, Ramsgate. This two-bedroom detached property is located in a popular residential area and now requires modernisation. The property has off-street parking, a gas central heating system, and part double-glazing. The garden is a particular feature, as it is where the remains of three ladies were discovered. They had all been slaughtered by a former owner during his occupation."

A photograph of the front of the property was quickly displayed on the screen. The cameraman was busy filming sections of the audience, making sure he zoomed in on the bidders, as the proceedings unfolded. Colin and Albert had settled in. They were waiting to bid on lot Forty-six. Albert would make the bids. The partners had already agreed the top price they were prepared to pay.

Colin and Albert were ignoring the display. They were conversing quietly.

"I didn't fancy this one," Colin remarked. "One thing I couldn't handle was the smell. I went over there, had a shufti around. Even after six months since the murders, there was a stink to the place."

151

"I don't think that was because of the remains," Albert chipped in. "They had been dug up from the garden."

"Well then, I am not sure what was causing the smell. The place had a right old pong!"

"Maybe just damp, Colin. It's been empty since they took Martin Cronie into custody. Did you know he topped himself two weeks ago?" Colin didn't think it was the smell of damp, but let the matter drop.

"I never knew that," said Colin. "Silly sod. Should never have perpetrated the crimes, should he?"

"Well," said Albert. "It takes all sorts!"

"Can I start the bidding at the guide price of eighty-five thousand?" the loud voice of Dominic Pilgrim boomed out across the conference room.

"Anyone in the room to start me at eighty-five? Eighty then. Eighty I have, I'm on the way."

An elderly man, in a grubby navy suit had held up his programme, and nodded to signify his bid.

"Eighty-two? I have eighty-two, eighty-four? The lady over there, with her leg in the air!"

Albert turned around to look in the direction of the lady bidder. He couldn't see any leg in the air. He did spot a blonde woman, in a bright red coat, waving her programme.

"Eighty-six. Can I say? Eighty-eight? Ninety? Do I have ninety-two? Ninety-four, It's back to you, sir."

The man in the navy suit, and the blonde, were bidding against each other. No one else had entered the contest. The man nodded and raised his catalogue once more.

"Ninety-six?" Red Coat never moved. Not an inch. No way would she pay more than ninety-two thousand. So she froze. She didn't want to risk moving a muscle. It might be misinterpreted as another bid. This was her first auction, and she didn't realise that Dominic Pilgrim was fine-tuned to bidding signals and would never make a mistake.

"No? Are we all done at ninety-four then? Ninety-four for the first time. Ninety-four for the second time. Ninety-four thousand pounds for the third and final time."

Dominic Pilgrim banged his wooden hammer on the top of the lectern. The screen displayed the closing price of ninety-four thousand pounds.

"Sold to you, sir, Your number? Nine zero five zero. Thank you, sir."

Navy Suit rose from his seat and shambled over to the door. He was off to pay his ten percent deposit on number 42 Coronation Drive, Ramsgate. He planned to move in a.s.a.p. He was single, had never had a woman in his life. Consequently, he was weirder than if he had experienced the delights of intimate female company. He wrote horror novels, but in recent years, he'd run out of ideas. He'd gone a bit in the head. He believed that living at 42 Coronation Drive might stimulate the old brain cells, give him ideas for his next book. It was a long shot, but he could afford to take the risk. His novels, including *Vampire Heaven*, had sold millions and had been translated into eight languages. *Cannibal Criminals* had been made into a film. Navy Suit may have been elderly and eccentric, but he was rich. If the house purchase didn't get him writing good stories again, well then, he would simply sell it on.

The display screen had changed its photograph. Another property was shown. Dominic Pilgrim continued the auction.

"Moving on to our next sale. Lots Forty-three and Forty-four have been withdrawn from sale. The former was sold prior to auction. The house that was to be lot Forty-four is to be demolished. The authorities have decided that the atrocities committed there were so awful that they want to wipe the place from the landscape. They do not want anyone moving in there and capitalising on the notoriety of the house and its former occupants. Our company appealed the decision to destroy the premises, but sad to say, we failed. This is doing us out of potentially good business, and is reducing the opportunities for our clients to indulge their passion for owning homes of horror. We are supposed to be living in a democracy, and I for one believe that this is another example of the erosion of our civil liberties. It is nothing less than a restriction on trade!" He looked around the room as if letting his words sink in.

"So, we come to lot forty-five. This is 58 Longdown Road, Canterbury. A two-bed, mid-terraced house having gas central heating and UPVC replacement double glazed windows. The property also comes with the benefit of laminate floors to the downstairs lounge. Underneath the lounge floor was found the body of a young male who was raped and murdered seven months ago. The body was in a decomposed state, but items of clothing with his name visible on sewn-in labels, verified the identity of the deceased, who suffered from bouts of memory loss. After the incident, the house stood empty for a short time, but a bunch of drugged-up squatters took it over, until they found out its gruesome history."

The auctioneer pointed to the image of number 58 Longdown Road.

"You know, it amazes me that so many people don't have the imagination to realise the financial possibilities of purchasing a house of horror. The fact is, as I am sure you all appreciate, and which is why most of you are here today, these places rent out for small fortunes to our wealthy clients who have a taste for the macabre. Buy one of our properties, and we will post you out our list of these people."

This was why Albert and Colin were at the auction. They had made a good business of buying homes with a history of violence, and tarting them up, always making sure to preserve the signs of the atrocities that had taken place on the premises. Colin, relatively new to the game, already owned three houses steeped in murder. Albert had a portfolio of twelve, having taken advantage of the growth of buy-to-let mortgages over the past five years. Building societies and some of the major banks had been falling over themselves to grant loans and had relaxed their lending criteria. Recently Colin and Albert had gone in together. Their partnership bought the places. Colin did them up. John Pilgrim and Sons provided the wealthy tenants and managed the properties. Everyone made money.

Albert owned an enormous house in south London that had been the scene of a number of beheadings by a bunch of terrorists. He was renting it to an Austrian film producer for five thousand pounds a month. Without its gruesome history, he would have achieved less than half that amount.

Dominic Pilgrim was off and running again.

"Start where you will on this one. Seventy-five thousand?"

No bidders to start.

"Seventy then, I won't go below seventy. Good. Seventy to the gentleman in the tweed jacket. Seventy-two, seventy-four can I say? Seventy-six I'm bid, seventy-eight I have. Eighty do you want to say?"

A number of bidders had raised their programmes. There was a lot of interest in this property. The bidding was with a thin young man in a leather jacket. Albert figured that he couldn't have been older than twenty-three. Then he thought he recognised him.

"Surely that's Phil Markham, from that rock group?" he said to Colin. "You know who I mean. What are they called?"

"Yeh," his partner replied. He too had spotted the young guy. "It is. It's the lead singer from 'The Cemetery'." 'The

Cemetery' played a cross between heavy metal, gothic stuff, and rap. They were the latest success story in the music business.

Dominic Pilgrim had reached a hundred and four thousand pounds.

"One zero four thousand," he called. "Give it a try. It's only money."

Phil Markham raised his programme.

"A hundred and six. Back to you, sir. You've stood with it for a long time."

A middle-aged albino had nodded his bid.

Markham nodded. "One zero eight to Mr Markham."

"A hundred and ten?" The albino raised his programme. "It's there to be sold."

"One hundred and twelve?" a guy with a mobile phone nodded yes.

There were now three bidders for number 58 Longdown Road.

"Remember the unusual underfloor feature. It's a bargain at a hundred and twelve. One hundred and fourteen?"

"It's with you, Mr Markham. One fourteen? It will be by the time we have finished with this one. I've won a game of snooker quicker than this. But not often!"

Albert checked his watch. It read twelve minutes past one. The bidding continued, one hundred and sixteen thousand pounds, one eighteen, one twenty.

Phil Markham had just nodded yes to one hundred and twenty thousand pounds.

Dominic Pilgrim went through the usual routine.

And finally, "One hundred and twenty, for the third time." The hammer had fallen. The deal was done. Phil Markham gave his number and left the hall to pay his deposit.

"We will have some wild parties there," he remarked to Alicia, his girlfriend. "I know a lot of people in the entertainment business who are attracted to places where someone has died in bloody circumstances."

"Can't wait," Alicia replied, squeezing his butt.

The proceedings moved on and lot Forty-six was next. Albert and Colin were keyed up for this one. They had looked it over, and felt that with the minimum of expenditure they could refurbish and rent it out for around two thousand a month.

"Lot Forty-six, A four-bedroom, double-fronted, detached house at number 32 Etherington Terrace, Orpington. The property comes with benefit of generous-sized rooms, including a large reception room, oil fired central heating, double-glazing, quarry-tiled kitchen and utility areas, double garage, and large garden. This is the property where some years ago, Winston Stanley hanged himself from a beam over the staircase. His body hung there, undiscovered, for three months. It was an especially horrifying experience for his daughter Rosalind who discovered the remains. Many of you know Rosalind Stanley, the world-renowned ice-skater, from her television appearances. More recently, a family of father, mother and four children, who occupied the premises, was murdered by a gang in what can only be described as a race killing. The guide price is one hundred and seventy thousand pounds. Who will start me off?"

Albert was silent. So was everyone else.

"One hundred and sixty then. Do I have one hundred and sixty?"

Still no bids.

"One hundred and fifty. That is as low as I am prepared to start." An impatient tone had crept into the auctioneer's voice.

Albert raised his catalogue.

"One hundred and fifty-five? One hundred and sixty, one hundred and sixty-five? One hundred and seventy. One seventy-five."

A bidder dropped out, and Albert found himself competing against a raven-haired woman in an expensive-looking fur coat. His eyes on the woman, Albert seemed annoyed.

"Just our luck. We might have to pay over the odds for this one. She looks as if she has a bob or two."

"One hundred and eighty? It's with you, sir."

Albert raised his catalogue, turning to face Colin as he did so.

"How high should we be prepared to go on this one? Can we do two hundred k?"

"One hundred and eighty-five." Miss Fur Coat hadn't budged. Albert was still turned away from the stage to hear Colin's answer. He absentmindedly raised his catalogue again.

"You're bidding against yourself, sir! Don't tempt me, sir. I am only an estate agent. If I were a politician, I would take your hundred and eighty-five!" There was a loud guffaw from the front row. Jimmy Brady, a local estate agent, clearly appreciated the auctioneer's joke.

"The bid is still one hundred and eighty thousand. Do I have one eighty-five? It's a bargain at one eighty."

"No? Am I going to let it go for one eighty?" The room was quiet. Albert and Colin held their breath. Was this to be their lucky day?

"One eighty once. One eighty twice." No one made a move. "One eighty thousand for the third and final time."

Dominic Pilgrim banged his hammer. Albert and Colin had bought lot Forty-six, the four-bedroom, double-fronted, detached house at 32 Etherington Terrace, Orpington.

They were surprised that Miss Fur Coat had dropped

out so soon. They didn't know that she was a friend of Rosalind Stanley who'd inherited the property from her late father and rented it out to the unfortunate victims of the race murders. Nor were they aware of what Miss Fur Coat knew about the premises. They were both happy in their ignorance. They'd expected to pay another fifteen grand at least. Colin and Albert raised their hands and did the high five.

"Whoooah What a great deal," said Colin.

"You bet it is. What a reeeeesult," Albert chimed in. "Let's pay the deposit and get out of here. I could do with a whisky."

So that's exactly what they did.

Albert and Colin spent a few weeks upgrading the property. They installed a complete new kitchen and bathroom, and new wood floors. Good quality, not the cheap laminate stuff. The whole place was redecorated, and they tidied up the garden. It was ready for renting, and it didn't take long before a tenant was found from the list provided by John Pilgrim and Sons.

Michael Page, an American businessman who spent a considerable amount of time in London, soon moved in at a rent of nineteen hundred pounds a month. He entertained a lot, and often his guests stayed over. Hence his preference for a four-bedroom property. He dabbled in the occult and the Black Arts. He liked to arrange séances to communicate with the spirit world. The American had been looking for some time for a property in which a hanging had occurred. It had been many years since Winston Stanley had taken his life. Michael Page was fascinated by the hanging and the circumstances surrounding the discovery of the body by the daughter. Michael was determined to invite her to one of his fancy-dress parties where the guests dressed as notorious murderers and their victims.

He was soon to hold a Jack the Ripper night. He'd seen Rosalind Stanley on the television and had taken a fancy to her, especially her thighs, another reason why he had wanted to rent the place. He was a horny bastard was Michael Page, and had a regular erotic fantasy of bedding the ice-skater in the room next to the landing where her father had taken his own life. The Ripper party didn't transpire, but Michael Page was a smooth operator and he did bed Rosalind, regularly as it turned out, but with little joy.

Everything seemed to be in order. Page had signed an Assured Shorthold Tenancy agreement, and arranged to pay the rent monthly by standing order. The house was let unfurnished and he'd promptly made several purchases to his taste, mostly modern items, from IKEA. Colin and Albert were delighted with the way things had worked out, and were already planning their next purchase, probably from another John Pilgrim auction.

A month went by, the next rent was due. It didn't appear in the bank account that Colin and Albert had set up for their rental business. A few more days passed and still no rent in the account.

Albert phoned Michael Page.

"I am just a little concerned that we don't seem to have received your transfer of this month's rent."

"I cancelled the standing order. I am sorry about this. I know I am tied to a month's notice, but I am afraid I cannot stay at 32 Etherington Terrace any longer. Did you not receive my letter?"

Neither of the partners had received any communication from the American tenant, and Albert told him so.

"Well, I am sorry. I am prepared to pay a cash sum in

lieu of notice. I am sure we can agree a satisfactory amount. How about four thousand pounds? That's just over two months' rent. It should compensate you for my breaking the Tenancy Agreement."

Albert Higgins replied that he would confer with Colin Mason, his business associate. He pressed the American on his reasons for vacating the premises.

"The house is haunted, that's why."

Albert was surprised to hear this, but he wasn't to be put off so easily.

"But we thought you were into all that occult stuff, and any way we'd no idea the place was haunted. Are you sure?"

"Positive," Michael Page replied. "There are a number of them, ghosts I mean. I don't mind them being ghosts. It's not that, not that at all. You are right. I am very much at home with anything to do with the occult, the spirit world. It's not the fact that they appear. It's when they appear, and what they like to do."

Albert didn't understand. "What do you mean?"

The American hesitated. "Well, you see. I recently met the daughter of the guy who hung himself all those years ago. Rosalind Stanley, the famous ice-skater. You must have seen her on television, a real little corker."

"Yes," replied Albert, "she is a looker, I agree. So what's the problem?"

"These ghosts," said Michael Page, "they are ruining my sex life." He was clearly embarrassed at such a personal confession. But Albert couldn't resist pressing him further.

"I guess it's really none of my business, but I still don't understand. How are they ruining your sex life?"

"It's like this. They appear whenever I am about to make love with Rosalind. They line up, all seven of them, gathered around the sides of the bed, peering down at the two of us. They just stand there and look. I reckon they are a bunch of voyeurs. I used to think I was a bit of an exhibitionist, but I just can't relax with them watching. Four of them are just kids. It kinda puts me off. You know what I mean, I am sure."

Albert grinned. "You should take Viagra mate. It works for me!"

The American brought the conversation to a halt, promising to pay the four grand and to vacate the property in the next few days.

Albert and Colin, curious about the ghosts, did some research, and discovered that the house did have a reputation for being haunted. They also found out that Miss Fur Coat was a friend of Rosalind Stanley. They suspected that she had appeared at the auction to bid up the price, and then dropped out.

They hadn't got a bargain after all. In fact, every time they let the property, the tenant moved out within a few weeks. Only the seven ghosts remained, though they rarely saw any good sex.

About the Author

Jeff Laurents moved from London eight years ago with his partner, Polly, to live in Kent, initially in Ramsgate, though they will soon be moving nearer to Sandwich, to live in the country. After a career teaching a variety of subjects including English, History, Film and Photography, Jeff is concentrating on his favourite interests of writing and photography. His often-macabre short stories combine elements of dark fantasy, horror and humour. He has published articles on film and photography and a short story.

Jeff has also written a novel, *The Music of The Spheres*, which he refers to, (tongue in cheek), as a spoof Sci-Fi/Fantasy/Horror/Musical/Love Story. He hopes to write two further novels as sequels. Jeff makes no apologies for being particularly motivated to write when he feels there is a chance of publishing interest. His novella, *The Backward Kid*, is being considered for publishing.

Jeff's fiction is influenced by authors, including Roald Dahl, Clive Barker, Stephen King and H.P. Lovecraft, but he is also indebted to his background, studying and teaching film. His stories can sometimes evoke the dark and angular imagery of film noir, while the movies of Fritz Lang and Alfred Hitchcock have also stimulated some of Jeff's approaches to his craft.

Jeff has also run a music business, sung semi-professionally, and currently runs his own photography business specialising in iconic scenes in Kent, photographic images he has manipulated to resemble paintings more than straight photographs.

Jeff has long been interested in transforming, rather than recording reality, and it is this concern that influences his writing in the direction of the edgy and weird.

Like to Read More Work Like This?

Then sign up to our mailing list and download our free collection of short stories, *Magnetism*. Sign up now to receive this free e-book and also to find out about all of our new publications and offers.

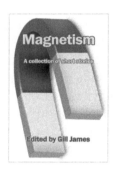

Sign up here:
   http://eepurl.com/gbpdVz

Please Leave a Review

Reviews are so important to writers. Please take the time to review this book. A couple of lines is fine.

Reviews help the book to become more visible to buyers. Retailers will promote books with multiple reviews.

This in turn helps us to sell more books... And then we can afford to publish more books like this one.

Leaving a review is very easy.
Go to https://smarturl.it/ien305, scroll down the left-hand side of the Amazon page and click on the "Write a customer review" button.

Other Publications by Bridge House

Resilience

by Jim Bates

Remembrance Day is special for one grandfather. Which story
of he and his brother at the lake will John remember today?
Blake loves his garden but he's not so sure about the rabbit.
Tyler stands up to his dad while hunting crows. What really
did happen in the room at the Inn on the Lake? Why doesn't
Quinn run away anymore?

"*Resilience* is an absolute gem. A collection of twenty-seven
beautifully written short stories that deal with the central theme
of its title." (Amazon)

Order from Amazon:

ISBN: 978-1-914199-00-4 (paperback)
978-1-914199-01-1 (ebook)

Whisky for Breakfast

by Christopher P. Mooney

The thirty-five stories in Mooney's debut are dominated by a cast of characters who colour outside of society's lines. They are hustlers, prostitutes, addicts, gangsters, killers, thieves, beasts. They are the dangerous, the lost, the lonely, the sick, the suicidal, the broken-hearted. Men and women, defeated by life. Their depravity is real, yet the writing in this uncompromising collection of transgressive fiction, always carefully crafted, evokes the sense that their humanity is not yet lost. In *Whisky for Breakfast*, nothing is off limits.

"A terrific read, often shocking and full of memorable characters. This is an excellent collection of short stories and would highly recommend." (*Amazon*)

Order from Amazon:

Paperback: ISBN 978-1-907335-89-1
eBook: ISBN 978-1-907335-90-7

In Fields of Butterfly Flames

by Steve Wade

Ostracised by betrayal, isolated through indifference, gutted with guilt, or suffering from loss, the characters in these twenty-two stories are fractured and broken, some irreparably. In their struggle for acceptance, and their desperate search for meaning, they deny the past. Some abandon responsibility, others are running from something or someone. Some flee their homes and their homelands, while others return home, only to find themselves even more marginalized and estranged.

"It's not too often when a book can make you physically react to the words. Haven't read anything as visceral, gripping and real as this in a long time... Highly recommend!" (*Amazon*)

Order from Amazon:

Paperback: ISBN 978-1-907335-87-7
eBook: ISBN 978-1-907335-88-4

Lightning Source UK Ltd.
Milton Keynes UK
UKHW021016231121
394456UK00013B/1084